Heart House
by Carey Lucki

This story would not exist today if it weren't for insomnia, Lake Huron and a wonderful little cottage. In 2009, I was given the opportunity to stay in a quaint little place named Heart House which was situated just off Lake Road on the shores of Lake Huron. It was during this unprecedented stay that I somehow became inspired to put this story on paper.

Heart House is as real as it gets.

The wooden heart still hangs on the front door and the sunsets continue to be spectacular.

I only hope you enjoy this story as much as I did.

FOREWORD

Some say that people who experience *punarbhava*—the entire process of change from one life to the next—are literally 'becoming again.' Wikipedia goes on to say that "within one life and across multiple lives, the empirical, changing self not only objectively affects its surrounding external world, but also generates (consciously and unconsciously) its own subjective image of this world, which it then lives in as 'reality.' It lives in a world of its own making in various ways. It 'tunes in' to a particular level of consciousness (by meditation or the rebirth it attains through its karma) which has a particular range of objects, a world available to it. It furthermore selectively notices from among such objects, and then processes what has been sensed to form a distorted interpretive model of reality: a model in which the 'I am' conceit is a crucial reference point."

So I suppose that this story is about my own distorted 'I am' conceit. As per Buddhist cosmology, my particular 'state of being' in the twenty-first century was destined. I can only surmise that my karmic deeds in a past life were treacherous enough to warrant all of this.

I must have tortured a past lover.

CHAPTER 1

If you were to ask about his prodigious talents at the time, I wouldn't have known what to say other than that he was special. Or so I had thought.

Maybe it had to do with the way his right cheek twitched when a teary-eyed woman requested more tissues.

"Excuse me, sir, but may I have another? The grief is really quite unbearable."

I had been watching this scene play out over and over as I stood in the frame of the doorway, wondering if he was truly empathetic or simply concerned about his tissue supplies.

"Ma'am?" He had walked over to me in the briefest of seconds. My bone-dry eyes had looked up as I sucked in my breath, suddenly happy to have a distraction from the melodramatic antics unfolding all around me.

"The name's Randy—Randy Dresser. I'm the funeral director." He held out his hand in a courteous way, and I could see the dark hairs sprouting from the tops of his pale knuckles. His navy suit was a beautiful contrast to his red silk tie.

"Ann Ralston." I extended my hand and his fingers immediately made contact.

"I know this is a difficult time for everyone." His voice was deep, and it amused me how he managed to force a smile and convey his glorious compassion at the same time. "But I think it would be most advantageous if folks start heading into the other room for refreshments now. Perhaps you wouldn't mind taking the lead?" He tilted his head ever so slightly in the direction of the reception suite. In a very strange way, this tiny gesture made me smile.

I stole a glance towards the casket, next to which my jittery boss, Frank Ellis, was standing. His head was not less than four inches from that of his poor dead mother, and his fingers stroked the polished wood like he was in a trance. I blinked and turned my attention back to Randy Dresser. Now it was my turn to tilt my head. He really was quite cute, and he still hadn't let go of my hand.

"It would be my pleasure."

He leaned in a little closer and I could smell a strong, woody scent with hints of bergamot. "That would be greatly appreciated. The family will require a private moment before we close the casket." He squeezed my hand and, as he smiled, a soft flutter escaped from my heart.

That had been exactly four years ago, and from that day forward we discovered significant pleasure in the back of his Chevy Venture, got engaged, spoiled ourselves with a quaint wedding of distinction, and finalized the entire package with a nasty divorce.

Now it was less than a week before Christmas and we were anything but amicable. In fact, I was on my way to the courthouse.

"Where to, ma'am?" The taxi driver looked like he hadn't shaved in four days.

"Old City Hall. Small claims, on Queen." My voice was flat and monotonous. I tried to focus on his ice-crusted windshield because I had no intention of making eye contact, let alone engaging in any conversation.

This night we pray,
Our lives will show
This dream he had,
Each child still knows

The Transiberian Orchestra was playing on the radio, and as I turned to stare out the window, the legato strokes from the violins embraced me with their beautiful sounds. A deep hollow pain tore through me. And yet *I* had been the one who had initiated the divorce.

By golly, Ann, what's wrong with you? My mother's words flooded back into my mind in vivid detail. *He's a fine man. Why, look at how he cares for the grief-stricken folks at the funeral home.*

Looking out the cab window at the passing Toronto streetscape, I tried to silence my mother's voice, along with the many other reproaches that tore at my heart and clawed at my guilt. I knew love could wax and wane even in good relationships, but somehow I also sensed that something much more serious was amiss in this one. Without any advance notice, the magic between Randy and I had just seemed to evaporate. From there it was a slow spiral downwards. In retrospect, I may have tried to rationalize that it was a mere case of infantile marriage, but clearly a missing link had existed from the beginning. My complete ignorance of this fact at the time only compounded the issue, and after a year of marriage, I became a separate entity and retreated from our relationship altogether. The two of us became ships passing in the night. Every night.

It's about finding someone compatible, Ann. It's about finding a good man who will provide for you— not some fairy-tale love connection that goes above and beyond reality. What on earth are you looking for?

My mother clearly equated marriage with sustenance—a means to an end, with strict outcomes and order. And I was to be chastised for wanting something more.

It had taken time, many appointments with my psychologist Dr. Harris, and some intense sessions of self-reflection, but I eventually came to the realization that it was *me* who had mistakenly created some sort of superficial love with Randy. He was a decent and attractive guy, sure, but the unfortunate reality was that I had not been in love with Randy. Not real love. And it was painful to realize, because all along I had known that we did not have that mutual and profound connection that, as Thomas Moore once said, is a product of divine grace.

I wiped a tear from the corner of my eye. How could I not have opened my eyes to this at the time? Was it a fault of my upbringing? I was suddenly awash with shame at my artlessness.

"Ma'am?"

I turned from the window.

The cab driver looked at me. He pressed his lips together before he spoke. "We're here."

I took in my surroundings as if for the first time. The cold gray stone, the daunting steps. I turned back to the cabbie, suddenly feeling desperately alone with nobody in the world but him as an ally.

"It'll be thirty-two dollars and I truly wish you a good day." He pressed his lips together again.

I couldn't help but admire his astute sensitivity.

CHAPTER 2

It was a short walk across the street to City Hall, but the winds were fierce and my eyes were tearing up again by the time I reached the main doors. I couldn't believe that I was going through this. Again.

Two years ago, the trials and tribulations of our divorce had created more stress and tears than I had ever imagined possible. But after months of dismal musing and trying to understand if I had done the right thing, hope had finally begun to surface. And then, eight months ago, Randy had decided to make my life a living hell yet again.

I approached the reception area, determined that Randy's heartless attack would end today.

"Dresser versus Ralston? Room four. Judge Caplan will be presiding. Please have all the necessary papers ready." The heavyset woman in her fifties spoke with such impassivity that I wondered how long she had been doing this job. I passed through a set of heavy wooden doors and the sweet smell of white freesia overwhelmed me. The wooden chairs were cold, and my body shivered as I tightly crossed my Wolford-clad legs in an attempt to create some aura of heat within me. Then I glanced across the room to where Randy was sitting.

I narrowed my eyes at him. Instead of settling for our simple and amicable divorce, he and his counterpart, Marion, had decided to go one step further and create financial havoc for me. They definitely deserved a medal for their dogged persistence, and obviously enjoyed the notion of toying with my guilt, for even after I had given up far more than an equitable share following the sale of our house and its contents, I was there that day because Randy had launched a second statement of claim for emotional damages. He was suing in the range of one hundred thousand dollars, and listed a host of blatant lies throughout the entire legal document.

I fumed as I sat on my cold chair. News travelled fast, and I knew he had moved north, bought an old decrepit funeral home, and was living on acres and acres of land with a local by the name of Marion. Marion worked as a cashier at Walmart, and although she was able to steal cigarettes and Twinkies, I'd heard that they were continually under the gun when it came to money.

I took a deep breath. Marion was here today, sitting extremely close to him. She was plumper than I imagined her to be, and she had a perm. She also seemed to have a way of tucking in her shirts and belting things a little too tightly, not to mention keeping her jaw slightly ajar when chewing gum. I wondered if this helped her to concentrate. *By the grace of God, what does Randy see in her?* I wondered. And yet, at that moment, Randy was displaying a tenderness towards her that I had never seen in our entire year of marriage. He wouldn't let go of her hand, and he seemed to take great pride in explaining legal terms to her. It was hard to believe they had mutually found that blessed bond, and in a trite way, I envied them. *Good for them to be so happy with each other while they're making my life miserable*, I seethed.

Mr. Panhwar, the dedicated concierge at my condominium, had tried to soften the blow before handing me the envelope back on that fateful spring morning all those months ago. "Mees Ralston? There was this gentleman in a very nice blue suit that came to drop this off today, and he said it was very, very important. He said that you must see this today and not tomorrow or the next day. I do not know who he is or where he came from, but he looked very serious. Yes, he looked very, very serious."

I remember watching him discreetly push a small paper plate under the lip of his security desk, lick his index finger, and then carefully pull a manila envelope from a stack of papers on his desk. The scent of curry permeated the lobby. I remember inhaling deeply while simultaneously noticing flecks of red curry paste glistening on his coarse white whiskers. I made no move to take the envelope from him. "Mr. Panhwar, your breakfast smells delicious."

He twitched ever so slightly at my remark as he held the envelope towards me, staring at me like I was on another planet. "Mees Ralston? The envelope?"

I looked intently at Mr. Panhwar. Every time we spoke, I couldn't help but think of the story he once told me about how he and his wife had struggled with competing schedules to raise two young children on their meager incomes since immigrating to Canada. I learned how they functioned as two silhouettes—she, with her evening shift at the airport, and he, beginning work in the middle of the night in our condominium complex. With a rusty Caravan as their primary mode of transportation, they had managed to run an efficient work schedule, though they barely saw each other.

I had felt badly when he told me that story, for they were enduring so much hardship. My face must have registered sadness, for he'd quickly patted my hand. "Mees Ralston," he'd assured me, "don't worry. We are happy to be in Canada and blessed to have each other and our family."

On that warm April day as I had watched Mr. Panhwar's wet whiskers twitch in concern above the envelope, I promptly did four things. I thanked him, took one last whiff of his delicious curry, and carefully slid the envelope under my arm. Then I found an upholstered velvet chair in the lobby and read the entire ill-fated document from start to finish.

I spent my morning this way. It had been difficult—not only trying to decipher the legal linguistics that lawyers often hide behind, but also doing my best to check my plummeting emotions under the concerned eyes of Mr. Panhwar. The entire experience had been draining. When I finally arrived at work, I didn't even lash out at anyone who crossed my path. Instead, I stayed morose. I was quiet and deflated, as though I had had enough. It was bad enough that Randy had led me on an exhaustive journey of playing cat and mouse games with lawyers throughout our lengthy two-year divorce ordeal, but now this? Where had I failed?

"I've heard enough. I'm ready to make my judgment." The words came to me slowly, as if underwater. "Will the defendant and plaintiff please approach the desk?"

A woman to my right lightly touched my forearm and brought me back to reality. "You'd better get up there before your ex starts up with something else." I looked up and my blurry eyes took note of a figure in a navy blue uniform nudging me forward. She had a pen in her right hand, and as I watched she ticked off a box beside the number 354. "Caplan is a stickler for time, and I can see that she's already getting impatient. She hates petty shit like this."

Managing to shuffle my frozen body into movement, I approached the desk that housed a stern-faced judge who looked like she could spew fire if provoked. She leaned forward towards Randy and lowered her glasses to the bridge of her nose.

"Mr. Dresser. You have already sued your ex-wife once. Do you realize that coming here a second time poses a certain degree of risk to you?"

Randy shifted his weight and grasped Marion's hand. He said nothing.

What did I ever see in him? I wondered.

The judge licked her lips and leaned in closer to Randy. "Judgement is denied, Mr. Dresser. Not only is your statement of claim invalid, but you have wasted a lot of time having me preside over this. I am hereby awarding Ms. Ralston a small settlement, in reverse to your claim, to make up for the stress and nonsense you have inflicted on her." She shuffled some papers on her desk hastily. "Case three fifty-four is closed. Next!"

There was a loud thump as her gavel made contact with her desk. I silently thanked the cosmos a million times over for putting an end to my eight months of misery. Marion and Randy were clearly not impressed, and it was wholeheartedly worthwhile to see the judge scold them. I promptly gave the kind security woman a small hug and, leaving the courtroom, I walked outside to embrace the wind and snow. As I smiled one of my first real smiles since the spring, I prayed to never set foot in a courthouse—or lay eyes on Randy Dresser—again.

CHAPTER 3

After five months had passed and the wind and snow were replaced by fresh apple blossoms, I made a conscious decision to devote myself to a long-neglected dream of writing. I was still slow to get over the recent episode with Randy, and Dr. Harris had indicated that putting down my thoughts in a few personal memoirs might be just the cathartic agent I needed to get me to the next level in my therapy sessions. I had every intention of continuing to work as a research assistant in my downtown Toronto firm during the week, and never imagined venturing beyond the city's borders on the weekends. But my arm eventually gave into the twist as I succumbed to the advice from one of my closest female friends, Renee Colter.

Renee was a real estate agent, and she had been encouraging me to buy a place in the country ever since Randy had dropped his lawsuit on me. Although the idea had seemed quite ridiculous at first, the thought of purchasing a property far from Toronto suddenly became quite appealing, if for no other reason than to provide me with peace and serenity when the city became venomous. And besides, I'd told myself, I needed a place that would give me a chance to write. It would be good for me—good for my soul, good for my body, and, most importantly, good for my mind. So I'd told Renee a few weeks ago to go ahead and start looking. And, two days ago, she'd called me to insist that she had discovered the perfect place for me.

We met at one of our favourite restaurants in Baldwin Village—a quaint café that had been transformed from a house. Renee was always late, and given that I arrived first, I requested to sit out back on their lopsided patio. It was overgrown with maples—a little antiquity reminiscent of old-town Toronto. The small back patio created an aura of unprecedented privacy that embraced me the moment I entered. The skies were crystal clear. I sank back in my chair and closed my eyes, savouring the warmth of the sun.

Within minutes, I could hear Renee's voice. She was still in the house, making her way towards the back, but I could hear her click-clacking heels on the ancient wood floor as well as her loud contralto as she greeted and chattered with everyone along the way. As usual whenever I was out with Renee, I was reminded of why she was such a success in the schmoozing business of real estate. When she finally emerged, I could only shake my head and smile.

Her thin frame looked dangerously balanced on her stilettos, and for a brief moment I wondered if she would fall or get a heel stuck in the uneven patio stones. Her black hair was stylishly straightened, and she was wearing one of her characteristic push-up bras with just a classy hint of flesh showing.

"You've lost too much weight, darling! Goodness!" she cried. As usual she was being far too dramatic, and people were now looking. With arms wide open, she dived in for the classic hug and kiss—although, for as long as I had known Renee, her lips never made contact with anyone's cheeks. Air kisses.

She stood in front of me with her hands on her hips and sized me up. "I can see your bones everywhere! Look at your collarbone—it's fantastic! You are looking so chic these days, like Jackie O or Carla Bruni. But, oh—" she tilted her head to the left "—perhaps with the fairness of Cameron Diaz." Diners on the patio continued to stare.

"Who the heck is Carla Bruni?" I asked as I looked down and realized I had spilled wine on myself.

She proceeded to stash multiple purses and shopping bags around her chair like a twisted cyclone. When she finally sat down, she heaved a loud sigh as she scanned for the waiter, anxious to order her classic martini. It was then that she clasped her hands over the table and leaned towards me. Her bangles hit her water glass in a chorus of chimes and she stared at me intently, pointing with one accusatory finger.

"Never mind Carla Bruni. Listen, I have found you the perfect place. It's right on Lake Huron and is absolutely fantastic. These cottages have been in the area for decades, and no one ever sells. Did you hear me? *No one.* These are cottages that stay in families for generations. This, my dear, is a rare find and we are going to snatch it." She slapped her hand on the tabletop so hard that I was surprised my wine didn't spill. And, of course, everyone was looking at us again. So much for the privacy. The waiter finally came and Renee ordered her martini with a straw. Lipstick perfection was always a must for Renee.

I refocused. "It must be expensive, then?" I ventured. "And old?"

"It's not expensive, honey—that's the best part about it. It's a very small cottage, yes, and it *is* a little old, sure—it was built in the forties. But it has a charm to it that you will *love*. I checked it out on the weekend and even *I* loved it. They call it Heart House. Isn't that adorable? There is this cute red heart on the front door, and if you look really closely, there are little hearts everywhere."

I was not sure I liked the sound of this. *Hearts? Little hearts everywhere?*

Renee must have seen the doubt in my eyes. "The property is key here, honey. The sunsets and beaches of Lake Huron are going to amaze you beyond words." She emphasized the word 'amaze'. "This is definitely a feel good place—and that's exactly what you need right now."

She pulled out a few photos from her purse and slid them across the table towards me. They were snaps of white sandy beaches and cloudless azure skies. I had to admit that the lake looked amazing. There was another photo of a cute blue clapboard cottage surrounded by pines.

"Is this it? Well, I'll admit it has a certain charm," I told her. "And it's right on the lake?"

"Right on the lake," Renee confirmed. "There'd be nothing around for miles except for you, the beach, and the water." She paused before correcting herself. "Okay, maybe not *miles*. There is a house next door." At that moment, Renee peered into her empty martini glass and quickly looked around for our waiter.

"How close is next door?" I asked, leaning forward.

She was staring at something in her glass, and I was getting impatient because I hated how her attention wandered like that. She waved her hand as if to dismiss me, bangles clinking. "Oh, stop worrying, Ann. It's like any regular cottage. I mean, it's not on your *doorstep*, if that's what you're asking."

I swirled the last little bit of wine in my glass. "I'm not particularly interested in being buddy-buddy with nosy neighbours for a while."

"Not *neighbours*, Ann. Try *neighbour*. And he's actually being a bit of a problem right now."

My senses perked up immediately. My eyes narrowed as I refocused my attention and stared hard at her. "And what the hell does that mean, Renee?" I desperately needed another glass of wine.

"Oh, relax." Renee began to push at her cuticles. "He just wants the property, that's all. I don't think he wants anyone moving in next door, so he's trying to scoop it for himself. Maybe to use it as a guest cottage or something."

The waiter finally came to our table and Renee ordered two glasses of Pinot noir. *Thanks, Renee. The first glass was a Shiraz. Did you even think to ask me?* "Great," I retorted. "So let's forget it then, okay? Because the last thing I need right now is another potential lawsuit." I moved forward in my chair and looked at her, my hands gripping the edge of the table. "And furthermore, even if there is no lawsuit, I don't want to move anywhere where the neighbour's inclined to make my life a living hell. I wouldn't be able to write, and it would all be a disaster. And I'm sick of disaster, okay Renee? I've had it for too many years, and I'm done with it. Okay? Done. Got it? And besides, it'd be just my luck that the guy could turn into some crazed axe murderer or something. Remember Deliverance?" I was speaking a mile a minute, and when I finally stopped, I noticed that Renee was staring at me with a slight look of irritation smeared on her face.

"Are you finished?" She sat back in her chair and crossed her long legs. I looked at her new shoes and decided that I didn't like them. They were a shade of deep purple, with a one-inch platform across the entire sole and a peep toe opening. She took a slow, long sip of her wine and smiled at me. I couldn't help but admire her astounding confidence, and yet she could easily be classified as a smug and annoying bitch. "I will get this for you. I'm the best there is, and I know people up there who owe me some favours. How do you think I found out about this cottage in the first place? Believe me, there will be no lawsuit and everything will be fine with the neighbour, okay? *Trust me.*"

CHAPTER 4

And so I trusted her. Within the week, I was the new owner of Heart House. The three-hour drive to Kincardine, which happened to be the nearest town to my new cottage, turned out to be quite the journey, given that I had never ventured into this stretch of Ontario before. And yet it felt strangely familiar to me at the same time. Renee had left a little history pamphlet on Kincardine when she had dropped off the key, and so I knew that Kincardine dated back to the late 1800s. Two Scots, Cameron and Withers, had landed by ship and discovered an Ojibwa community by the name of Penetangore. They understood the community's name to mean 'river with sand on one side,' and they must have really liked the beach atmosphere because before long other Scots were infiltrating the area with specks of tartan and calling the place Kincardine.

Not long after I entered Grey-Bruce County, I was met with a welcome sign that seemed to say it all: Where You're a Stranger Only Once. *Well, let's hope so*, I thought.

My Audi passed through small towns bearing the names of Hillsburgh, Glammis, Clifford, and Teeswater, many dating back to the late eighteen hundreds. These little towns bore the remains of old town halls, post offices, and a surprising number of red brick churches—sometimes it seemed that there were almost as many churches as there were houses. There was a spattering of small, century-old cemeteries sprinkled between townships, and roadside stands selling apples and squash seemed to be at every intersection. Family farms had names such as Sydenham and Lorilee painted in large white letters across fading, dilapidated barns, and tall silver silos sparkled in the sun. Lily pads slept peacefully on stagnant ponds, while cows, sheep, and horses grazed on lush green patches of countryside. The drive had an incredibly calming effect on me, and before long my shoulders were feeling relaxed and all thoughts of my city-life problems were out of my head.

I recalled how Renee had told me that once I caught sight of the numerous wind turbines, I would be nearing my destination. Within minutes of that passing thought, they came into view. And they were everywhere. They appeared like an army of soldiers standing at attention, their massive white arms propelling in unison. As I came to a stop at a four-way, I found myself feeling utterly dwarfed by them. It was only when a truck driver honked his horn behind me that I realized I had been in a daze, like a child watching a Christmas tree light up for the first time.

Feeling embarrassed, I pulled into a nearby parking lot. The gravel crunched loudly under my tires, and a small breeze cut through the late-September humidity as I stepped from my car. A swirl of dust and gravel swept by my face and I welcomed the grimy feeling. It reminded me that I was far away from Toronto—and far away from all the stress that had been building there.

I blinked a few times to clear my eyes, and when I was able to see again, I found that I was standing in front of a one-storey white building with an ancient rusty sign dangling from the eaves and screeching in the wind. *McKellars General Store.* Nothing more could be heard.

There were three steps leading to an old porch where bags of firewood were stacked. As I walked up the steps, my hand self-consciously felt my hair, which was wild and wavy with the humidity. As I pulled a stray piece away from my face and tucked it behind my ear, I could hear a dog yelp in the distance. There was a stillness about the place that made it seem like some forgotten moment in time. The store had one of those old-fashioned screened doors that groaned as I opened it, only to release a quick and hard slapping noise that made me jump upon entering. I quickly looked up to apologize for the noise, but I saw nobody behind the counter.

Is anybody here? I wondered, half expecting somebody to be playing the banjo on a back stoop to complete the image. *Stop it, Ann.*

The small store had a bit of a musty smell, but as I looked around, I realized that it was amazingly organized and the selection was impressive. I decided that this was as good a place as any to pick up a few things before trying to find my new weekend retreat.

"Good evening, ma'am." I nearly jumped out of my skin at the sound of the gentle male voice. I turned to find a man in his sixties with a slight limp carrying a case of paper towels. He had a full head of white hair and was wearing dark-rimmed glasses. He reminded me of my father. "Just let me know if you need a hand with anything."

I smiled in response. He had a way of making me feel immediately at ease. I picked up a small wicker basket from a stack near the door and began to fill it. Once I gathered my things, I approached the front cash, where I was met by the smiling face of a woman who appeared to be a few years younger than the man.

"How are you, dear? It's so damn hot and humid out there for September, eh?"

As I nodded in agreement, I studied her face. She had to be the gentleman's wife, I figured. Her hair was short and gray, and she had many wrinkles, but there was a beautiful rosy sheen to her face that made it possible for me to imagine her as a girl. I wondered if she had spent her whole life here.

"Are you visiting Kincardine?" She smiled with such sincerity that it made me feel like warm honey inside.

"Well, yes and no." I shifted my feet and felt nervous. "I actually bought a property near here, on Lake Huron."

Immediately her eyebrows went up. "Is that so! Where?"

"Um, on Lake Road," I offered. "I'm actually heading there for the first time now."

Her eyes immediately widened. "Oh, so *you* must be the city lady who bought the little cottage beside Jaime!" She said this with a combination of relief and excitement in her voice.

"Pardon?" I stammered. Surely it wasn't *that* small a town that she could figure out from what little I'd said that I'd bought Heart House.

But my confusion was lost on her as she gestured for her husband to come over. "Bob! This is the new owner of the cottage beside Jaime's," she explained. Understanding immediately dawned on her husband's face.

"Who's Ja—" I began, but I was cut off.

"We're the McKellars, sweetie," the kindly lady explained excitedly, turning back to me. "Everybody knows us. I'm Fran, and this is Bob. Bob has lived here his whole life, and I've been in the area for about thirty years now. We've known Jaime since he was just a baby."

"I'm Ann," I said. "Ann Ralston. So pleased to meet you." I held out my hand, but in doing so knocked a gum rack off their counter. "Oh, I'm so sorry!" I spoke to the floor as I scrambled to pick up wayward packages of Dentyne. At the same time, I couldn't help but wonder who this 'Jaime' was and how he figured into the conversation.

"Oh, he's such a wonderful boy, eh, Bob?" Fran gushed, and I wondered if she was still speaking about Jaime. "A police officer, you know. Quite high up in the ranks, I think."

I got back to my feet and hastily tried to replace the gum rack as it had been. Embarrassed, I did my best to straighten my hair.

"Here you go, dear," said Bob as he pushed the paper bag over the counter. "That'll be twenty-eight fifty."

I fumbled in my wallet for two twenties, and as Bob counted out my change I listened to Fran recounting how beautiful the stretch of shoreline along Lake Road was.

"How far is it from here?" I asked as I pocketed my change.

"Not far at all," said Fran. "Ten minutes at the most. And Heart House is a gem—you'll love it!"

So it *was* a small enough town that they knew I'd bought Heart House. I picked up my grocery bag and wished the McKellars goodnight. As I walked slowly to my car, I couldn't help but think that the welcome sign had said it all. *I guess people really are strangers only once.*

CHAPTER 5

The drive along Highway 21 was quiet, and as I watched the countryside slowly transforming in the dusk, I was lulled into a near trance. The darkness set in quickly as I struggled to find the address that Renee had given me. Before long the night was heavy and silent, its blackness breathing and breeding without the constraints of city lights.

I began to feel apprehensive, as I had no experience driving on dark roads in cottage country. I was getting frustrated. Could they not afford to put up more signs here? Just when I was beginning to think that I would be sleeping with the chirping crickets, I finally found the cottage virtually hidden behind a crop of huge pines.

As I pulled in, my headlights lit up the front of the little building. Immediately, all of my mounting frustration dissolved into the silent night air. The little cottage couldn't have been more than eight hundred square feet, but it was clearly a sturdy structure that had withstood the test of time. It had a large stone chimney snaking up one side of the building, which lent a simplistic yet warm appeal to the house that placated me. As I stepped out of my car, I looked up to see the stars smiling back at me. Or at least it seemed that way.

I made my way to the front door, key in my trembling hand, and smiled when I saw that the wooden heart was in its place, just as Renee had mentioned. Spider webs graced the eaves and, once I opened the door, the strong smell of cedar hit. Renee had boasted that the cottage had been built with this magnificent sweet-smelling wood, but I never imagined that the fragrance would have remained so succulent. With my fingers splayed and both hands navigating the walls, I searched for the lights in vain.

I paused. Standing in the dark in the middle of what must be my kitchen, I reminded myself that this was the start of my 'new' life. A better life. "Things will be good," I whispered to the darkness, trying to convince myself. And yet, at the very same time, I was experiencing a terrible pang of loneliness laced with a trace of fear.

Loneliness is not the experience that one lacks, but rather the experience of what one is. These words came to me from somewhere in the furthest reaches of my mind. I reflected on Michele Carter's view as I searched and eventually found the light switch.

When the cottage lit up with warm light, I gasped. Besides seeing a few pictures of the landscape, I had never laid eyes on the interior of the place and had relied completely on Renee to find something that would suffice. All I had requested was a place that would allow me to repent my sins and spend my weekends somewhere where I could write in peace—and perhaps even inspire me. As I looked around the place for the first time, I could see that Renee had done well, and that I owed her.

Off the very small kitchen was the primary living space, which was simply endearing with a rustic Gustavian English country style. The walls had been tastefully whitewashed to maintain a sense of freshness in the interior. Aged cedar planks mixed with varnished pine made up the floors, and the spruce ceiling had darkened considerably with age and dripping sap. The evening atmosphere was dark and moody, but nevertheless tranquil. The huge fireplace, clearly the focal point of the room, had a beautiful barnboard mantel topped with matching Scandinavian candelabras. The iron screen in front of the fireplace was flanked by tidy piles of fresh-cut logs, and antique sideboards graced the perimeter of the room. Baskets, flowers, and plenty of books were everywhere.

Nice touches, Renee.

I ventured up the small and rickety staircase and found a fresh bedroom awash in serene blues and whites. The floors and walls had been bleached with a soft semi-opaque stain and an antique blue and white quilt lay over a plush duvet.

I headed back downstairs to the living room. The wall opposite the fireplace was essentially all windows, with a French doorway that led out to what seemed to be a deck area. Though there was not much of a view to enjoy in the pitch darkness, when I opened the doors and heard the water so close by, I was thunderstruck.

There was a fair wind, and the sound of the waves crashing onto the shore somehow made me feel insignificant and small. It was like there was this portentous existence outside my door, and I had to be careful. It was a definite triumph and yet, all of a sudden, I was overcome with fear. I had spent the last three years of my life feeling alone and helpless inside, and I was coming to the lake to get away from that feeling. But suddenly, here it was again—the same, and yet different. Immediately I began to question the rationale of buying this property, and wondered if it had all been a stupid and impulsive mistake.

I grasped the door to keep me steady. *Put it away. Let it go*, I kept telling myself. *Breathe*. It took several minutes, but I managed to pull myself together. There had been too many years of strife already. All I could do now was make a commitment to myself to be strong. The water and wind would be my friends and protect me. I promised myself that I had nothing to worry about as I walked back to the small kitchen. *You can do this, Ann.* I did my best to convince myself.

The cozy, unfitted country kitchen drew me in and brought an immediate sense of comfort. Spruce floors supported a 1930s electric stove and an extensive sideboard that was somehow fitted with a porcelain sink and modern plumbing. The antique pine table called out to me, and I sat down on one of the mismatched chairs and sighed. The kitchen window was ajar and I opened it further, causing the light cotton panels to flutter in tandem with the wind. Remarkably, the place gave me the familiar feeling of being there before, yet I could not place it.

Was it déjà vu?

Strange, I thought. *It's almost like I've been here before... It reminds me of a place my mother might have taken me.* I struggled to think back to when I was very young, maybe five or six years old, and my mother and I used to jump into the old station wagon and take off for weekend trips at the drop of a hat. *Just us girls*, she'd say. That train of thought slowly evaporated as my mind came back to the present.

I smiled at the small pots of lavender that graced the wooden countertop, and was reminded that I had friends like Renee who would see me through this.

It was then that I decided that Heart House was a keeper.

CHAPTER 6

As I descended the stairs on my first morning at Heart House, the view through the French doors took my breath away. Steely blue Lake Huron was no more than fifty feet away, and between the cottage and the water lay a strip of fine white sand.

Last week's Kincardine Independent was lying on my kitchen table basking in bright sunlight. After making a pot of coffee, I poured a cup and set it down on the section that read 'Subscribe to the Independent'. My eyes scanned over to the editorial page, where a smattering of letters conveyed strong emotions about the wind turbines. I read through a few and discovered that long-time residents of the area were clearly not impressed with these energy-producing contraptions. It was a large and complex topic that mixed health and environmental issues into one, and residents were deeply concerned about the potential for the turbines to lower property values. As one letter pointed out, National Geographic had cited Lake Huron as being one of the five best places on earth to view beautiful sunsets, and yet huge, flickering blades were taking over the skies.

The window was still open from last night, and the sound of the water made me look up from the paper.

It produced the same effect on me as Mozart's Violin Concerto Number Five, and it put me at ease immediately. In fact, last night's feelings of being overwhelmed had completely disappeared. The billowing white curtains were dancing in front of the kitchen window, and I wondered if this was how Francesca had felt in Madison County the day her husband and children had left for the county fair. With a silly giggle at my own thoughts, I glanced out towards the lake and immediately froze. There was a man standing on the beach—and a very handsome man at that.

Is this the neighbour? I wondered. I thought back to Fran's comments the night before, and my curiosity overcame me. *Jaime*. Within a moment I had managed to park myself beside the window and was peering out like an eighty-year-old woman with dementia. He had what appeared to be an eighteen-foot catamaran pulled up on the beach, and the next moment he was bent over doing something to his boat that resembled rigging. Whatever the case, he was clearly immersed in whatever it was he was trying to accomplish.

I walked back to the counter to get more coffee and returned to the window. Looking out again, I could see that he was in his early to middle thirties. Definitely younger than me, and probably by almost ten years. I figured him to be about six feet tall, and he had a strong, muscular build. I moved to the other side of my window to get a better view. *Please don't catch me peering out at you like I'm a raving lunatic*, I prayed.

He was wearing a pair of worn jeans and a pale blue button-down shirt rolled up to his elbows. Overall he had a slightly rugged look, but then he also appeared to be clean-cut and neat, which was surprising. His clothes seemed to fit him perfectly, with defined lines and angles marking the outline of his body. As he continued rigging the catamaran, I had to admit that his physique was quite remarkable. No doubt exercise was the norm for him because his shoulders were broad and nicely articulated, with a prominent band of musculature that extended up towards his neck. As my eyes trailed his arms, I couldn't help but notice the contour and bulk of his forearms. My hand found its way to my throat as I sucked in a little breath. There was a hint of shadow on his chiselled jaw. He had not shaved this morning.

At that moment, he looked up and out towards the horizon. I wondered if he was checking the viability of sailing. He ran his hand through his windblown hair. It was longer than I would have expected for a man of the law, and I was curious as to how he got away with that. He seemed pensive as he looked back down to his boat and tried to configure some device that was on the starboard side. I admired his diligence, and a smile emerged on my lips as I realized that he was not at all what I had originally made him out to be. Yet, in a very discrete and singular way, he definitely piqued my interest.

I raised my mug to take another sip of coffee just as he looked up and stared right in my direction. I stepped back at once, tripping over a bench in the kitchen that I could have sworn hadn't been there before. The coffee spilled everywhere, splashing on my bare arms and down onto the floor. I swore. I was certain that he hadn't seen me—he was likely only looking at Heart House in a random way—but my heart was racing nonetheless. A burning feeling was beginning to fester on my forearm, but I stayed slumped against the bench, drenched in a splatter of liquid and thinking about this stranger who apparently lived beside me.

A lovely man, Fran had said.

And no axe murderer, that's for sure.

CHAPTER 7

The rest of Saturday was uncharacteristically balmy for September. I spent two hours moving from window to window inside my little cottage, watching my neighbour on the beach. I was frightened to death that he would somehow see me spying on him, which necessitated an intricate stakeout plan from my end, but I could not keep myself from watching him; he had a strange pull over me. When he finally left the beach around noon, I heaved a sigh of relief. The heat was becoming unbearable in my own little cottage and I desperately needed fresh air, but I hadn't been willing to venture outside and risk a conversation with this stranger while he was clearly occupied on the beach.

I ran to my bathroom to pull my hair up off my sweltering neck and paused in the doorway to once again admire the small space. Instead of being confronted by a used and mouldy bathroom, I was met with a beautiful marble-topped vanity complete with a pretty, old-fashioned skirt in Tudor rose fabric that hid the plumbing and the toiletries. The same semi-opaque stain that graced the wooden panelling throughout the cottage reached its way into this room, giving it a clean and airy feel. Two antique fixtures hung on each side of the mirror, and fresh calla lilies were arranged in a white tin pail alongside the antique soap dish, filling the room with a tremendous scent. I was beginning to think that Renee should switch careers and become an interior designer when I caught a glimpse of myself in the mirror.

I registered a fanatical need to ensure I looked good today, and then a hearty laugh erupted from my lips as I realized how supremely ridiculous I was being. Here I was, for some reason hoping that I was going to run into my neighbour when I had just spent the last two hours doing everything in my power to avoid him. I could only marvel over how crazy women could get. Either that, or I was becoming despondently old.

I stepped through the French doors on the backside of my cottage and onto the large wooden deck and breathed in the scent of the lake. *I could get used to this*, I decided. From this main deck, there were three steps down to a second platform that jutted out towards the water. The deck planks were arranged on a diagonal, which definitely gave it a distinguished look. On the left side of the lower deck was a small concrete patio area that was surrounded by beautiful perennials and a gate.

The gate opened onto warm, white sand and showcased a well-used path leading to the water. Grasses and reeds grew tall and flanked the sides of the sandy path, and monarch butterflies flew everywhere. I looked around and counted at least twenty trees surrounding the back patio, including one large pine that came right through the floor of the upper deck.

Someone certainly had the decency to spare its life when the deck was being constructed some time ago.

Leaves and needles had begun to fall, and the colours on the ground left a pretty mosaic. The sun was warm, and although the wind had picked up, the breeze embraced my skin. The silence was marred only by the sound of the waves crashing against the shore and the leaves crunching under my steps. Occasionally I could hear a seagull in the distance, but my eye could not see any other living creature for miles. It was all so wonderful that I immediately felt good again. I couldn't help but wonder at how being with nature somehow resonated with the soul. *How have I stayed away from this for so long?* I wondered, already dreading my return trip to the city.

The sound of the water drew me to the shoreline. I had fight my way through a few overgrown pine boughs and cedar branches, but the waves were strong and their breaking sounds against the wet, sandy ground continued to guide me. As I reached the shore I watched the water roll in and out, the cool waves lapping at my ankles and my toes intermittently disappearing and reappearing in the sinking sand. I began to walk along the water's edge, my footsteps disappearing behind me. It was remarkable how smooth and pristine the wet sand became after every roll of the water.

My eyes rested on the catamaran that was lying on the beach. My gaze lingered towards the bush line and a second well-defined path that led through the reeds. Although there were a few trees that afforded some degree of privacy, I could definitely make out some details of a house. It seemed to be a large two-storey structure that had some interesting angles and architecture to it. My little cottage, quaint as it was, did not appear to be any match for this more contemporary structure. It stood quite a distance from where I was standing—a good one hundred yards at least.

My eyes scanned the area and discovered that there were four Muskoka chairs set up in a circle surrounding what appeared to be a bonfire pit. What interested me more was that the chairs appeared to be midway between my property and his. *Who do these belong to?* I wondered. *I might have to call Renee later.*

It was nearing lunch time and I was beginning to feel hungry, but I continued to stare at his cottage. I couldn't help but wonder if there was a connecting path between my place and his. *Get a grip, Ann. Enough.*

I turned my back on both cottages and found a nice patch of dry white sand about four feet from the shoreline. Pulling my knees up to my chest, I stared out at the great expanse of the lake and the unyielding horizon as the waves lapped their melody. An unmistakable calm overcame me, comparable to the feeling of being swayed back and forth like an infant in a mother's embrace. I thought back to how this very same embrace had frightened me only the night before, and I laughed at my own silliness.

Lake Huron, as unfamiliar and ominous as it had appeared at first, was going to be my new best friend.

CHAPTER 8

I didn't see him for the remainder of the weekend, and that bothered me a lot.

As I drove along the stretch of endless highway and farmland on my way back to the city, I kept wondering if he'd actually left, or if he just hadn't come out again. I hadn't seen any lights through the trees on Saturday night, but maybe our cottages were just too far apart. There was also the faint possibility that he had seen me peering out at him from behind my kitchen curtains and thought I was nuts. I gripped the steering wheel tighter. *Did he see me while I was on the beach? Why didn't he come out to say hello and introduce himself? Is he still mad that I bought Heart House instead of him?* My mind kept going in these same circles until I turned up the radio and forced myself to concentrate on the music. I really had to get a grip.

Just when my eyes were beginning to adjust to the dull countryside, a sudden scream leaping from my purse made me nearly jump out of my skin and swerve into a ditch. When the unfamiliar and wretched tone repeated itself, I realized that my sweet nephew must have adjusted the ring tone on my cell phone yet again. As I tried to breathe and get my heart rate back to normal, I made a mental note to refrain from allowing

Jonathan to play with my phone ever again. Speaking as calmly as I could, I answered the call.

"Hey honey. It's Rain."

I smiled. Back in elementary school I had decided to call Renee 'Rain'. It was such an innocent and sweet time back then, before the perils of adulthood and relationships struck.

"So, how was it?"

"Renee, it's beautiful, just like you said it would be. I can't thank you enough. The water is spectacular, and I love the cottage. It's perfect—exactly what I need. It feels just like home. In fact, I actually felt like I'd been there before. Renee, you really are a gem for finding this."

"Didn't I tell you so? And hey, did you run into the neighbour? I happened to catch a glimpse or two of him when I was up there getting things ready, and he looked yummy!" She drew out the last word. *Yum-my*.

"No, I didn't meet him. I only saw him briefly on Saturday morning. He was on the beach, working on his boat. That was it."

"And he was yummy, right?"

My phone began cutting in and out. "Renee, are you there? You're cutting out and there's a lot of static."

"—gorgeous." She was back. "I can't believe you didn't introduce yourself. Hell, I can't believe that *I* didn't introduce myself."

I could feel the heat on my cheeks and I felt the familiar sensation of being annoyed by Renee. "For Christ's sake, Renee. How many times do I have to say this? I am not entirely up for meeting a man right now, no matter how cute he is. Okay?"

"He's not just *cute*, Ann. He's gorgeous. Admit it."

I ignored this last comment. "And besides, considering that the guy wanted to buy the property that I bought, I'm sure the last thing he's looking for is to have a nice friendly chat with me."

There was another silence, and by now I was ready to hang up on Renee. I stared at some homes along the stretch of the highway and wondered about the flagpole obsession up here. I did not need this conversation right now. Not to mention that I was gripping the steering wheel with far too much tension after having gotten myself all worked up over some complete stranger whom I had never met.

I was determined to end the conversation there. "Look, my battery's about to die. I've got to let you go, Renee."

"Okay, darling, but drive carefully. I'll give you a call at the end of the week. Love ya."

The line went dead, and after throwing my phone on the front passenger seat, I stared intently out the window at a bunch of Holsteins grazing. I had a very faint feeling that somehow my life was not going to run smoothly at this cottage.

CHAPTER 9

It was the first weekend of October, and even though autumn had officially arrived, the weather gods must have decided that we deserved something special, as the forecast continued to call for warmer-than-usual temperatures for this time of year. As I drove up to the cottage on Friday afternoon, I mildly regretted that I hadn't invited some of my friends up to see the place, but I'd also wanted to secure some time for writing. This weekend had to be the start if I was ever going to initiate some self-discipline.

I turned onto Highway 21, and as I made my way towards Lake Road, a contemporary plaza on the outskirts of Kincardine came into view. A new motel had been built alongside a take-out coffee joint and across the road was a liquor store. I couldn't help but smile. As far as I was concerned, writing and sunsets required alcohol, and in no time at all I was standing in the check-out line with a bunch of red-faced Scots, clutching two bottles of wine to my chest. I had been fumbling in my purse for my wallet when I overheard a loud, hearty voice.

"Jaime! How are you, my good man?"

Even without looking I recognized the familiar man-slapping sounds. I stepped to my right and peered around the old woman standing in front of me.

"Good, Greg. Everything is pretty good. How's Susan?"

I managed to make another postural shift and it was then that I realized just how amazing the adrenaline hormone truly is. For no apparent reason my heart began to beat like I was running a footrace. I couldn't even begin to understand what the hell was wrong with me. Why on earth was I reacting like this? Then suddenly my eyes registered my gorgeous neighbour only a few people ahead of me in line, talking to the cashier. *There he is. Up close. Three feet away.* I actually felt like time stood still for a moment as I watched their little conversation unfold. I was severely transfixed, and could only marvel that other women had to feel the same way whenever they laid eyes on him. His beautiful hands were on the counter, and he was gesturing with one of them as he helped the so-called Greg bag his purchases with the other. He shifted his weight from one foot to the other, smiling as he talked. His teeth were essentially perfect. There were sharp contours to his face that were accentuated by his characteristic five o'clock shadow. He was a pretty boy, but rugged too. It was an odd combination, and yet, in a strange way, that was what made him so perfect.

I felt like I was being sucked in by his aura. Never mind that he was physically beautiful, or that his little impromptu gestures somehow pulled a trigger. All I could surmise was that there was something going on here beyond the obvious. My sister Thea, ever so vocal in her spiritual ways, would say that he was a type of 'enlightened' being, and I wondered if it was worth a call to discuss the issue in depth with her.

"Ma'am?"

I came back to reality and realized that I was standing in front of Greg, still hugging my bottles to my chest like they were the last ones in the store. Jaime was nowhere to be seen. I wondered how long I had been holding up the line.

"Ma'am?" Greg said, pointing towards the counter. "I need to scan them. Can you put them on the counter, please?"

Flustered, all I could do was smile. "Oh, sure." I placed the bottles on the counter and felt my cheeks flush as I casually glanced sideways at the line behind me. I couldn't be sure, but everyone appeared to be staring, like they knew I was in a catatonic state. I shifted my eyes, looking for Jaime. Where had he gone so quickly?

"Ma'am?" Greg's tone was beginning to reek with annoyance.

I snapped my head back around. "Um?"

"I *said*, that will be twenty-seven fifty." Had he said that for the second or third time?

"Sorry about that." I laughed, but it was a nervous laugh. "Long week. I'm just glad it's finally

Friday." I made a move to open my wallet, but it was upside down and coins spilled everywhere.

Greg winced and I could have sworn he rolled his eyes. I hurried to retrieve as much of my change as possible, and then held out two twenties. Greg didn't meet my eyes as he handed me the difference and wished me a good weekend.

Stupid city girl.

I grabbed my wine and rushed out the door, nearly tripping on the curb on my way out. I was completely disoriented and unable to find my car. Good lord, what had come over me? I closed my eyes and took a deep breath, and yet it seemed like such a long time before I was finally able to regulate my central nervous system and get my heart rate and breathing under control. After I had calmed down slightly, I located my car and yanked open the door. I felt like I needed a swig of the wine I'd just bought, but instead I threw the bag on the seat beside me and heard the bottles chime against one another.

I stared at my reflection in the rear view mirror. This was crazy. I sighed, closed my eyes again, and let my head sag against the head rest. It was too warm, and I was overdressed, and sweat began to trickle down in places I didn't like. I also began to chide myself for acting like a complete idiot in the liquor store. I pulled myself together enough to begin to analyze what had happened. My sick, desperate mind must have somehow built Jaime up to be something he wasn't—something no man could possibly be.

Yes, he was handsome, but I had seen handsome men before. There had to be a different reason for my reaction. I took a deep breath and made a mental note to discuss this with Dr. Harris at our next session. Was I simply bored after the past four years of turmoil and needing to create drama where there was none? Maybe I was emotionally empty or sex starved? I hadn't been with a man in so long that perhaps I was in some sort of hormonal withdrawal. And yet, there was a very small voice deep inside of me that seemed to beg for air—that needed to be listened to.

It seemed to say, *It's something more.*

Perhaps my physical responses were a by-product of something greater? Was this what love was—was this that elusive entity that had been so obviously missing between Randy and me? After all, wasn't love—real, true love—supposed to sneak up and appear out of nowhere, seizing you when you least expected it to? I hadn't even met the man. But maybe, just maybe, I had to believe.

At that moment I looked up. Directly in front of my car, a mother took her child's hand and crossed the parking lot. The child was holding a pink balloon emblazoned with an image of cupid and her arrow. I blinked. Twice. Was I really seeing this?

CHAPTER 10

Saturday came and the wine remained unopened. I couldn't bear to drink it after my silly ordeal in town. Instead, I crawled in for an afternoon nap and promptly fell asleep in what I decided was the most comfortable bed in the world. My confused emotions left me exhausted. Even though I awoke in the middle of the night, the sound of the water lulled me back to sleep and my body had no difficulty complying with the offer. And now it was mid-morning and I was still wrapped like a cocoon in my duvet. My thoughts were scattered, but there was a slight, constant nagging sensation that was telling me I should be writing.

In all truth, writing was turning out to be harder than I'd thought. I had the space, the peace, and the solitude, sure, but the mere task of placing my butt in front of my laptop and getting started was not working out the way I had planned. I was beginning to have doubts as to whether the stillness of the countryside would be enough to change my thinking. It certainly wasn't easy with the distraction that lived next door, and yet I knew that I desperately needed to overcome my writer's block. I turned to the window and felt a stream of warm air brush past me.

Why, of course. The beach…

Thirty minutes later I was at the water's edge, being spurred on by the thought of taking a long walk along the stretch of the shore. Last weekend I had noticed an assortment of people, dogs and children in tow, trekking across my beach in various stages of play, solitude, and romance, and I had panicked, thinking that there was some sort of public beach adjacent to my property. However, as Renee explained without her usual condescending tone, the beach in front of my place was part of a larger beach that went on for miles—halfway up the Bruce Peninsula, to be exact—and though the public could not be kept off private waterfront, there had rarely been any problems between the cottagers and the beachgoers in the past. "So don't be alarmed if someone strolls by in front of your cottage," she'd explained patiently, seeming all-too-aware of my recent fragile state. "The beach is for everyone, Ann. Everyone shares it and it's always been that way."

It was no mystery why people were drawn to that stretch of beach. Lake Huron was famous for its shorelines, along with its warm shallow waters and its beautiful sunsets. Renee advised me that some sections would be rocky, but then miles and miles of sand would appear out of nowhere. She also told me about a special beach called Singing Sands on Dorcas Bay. It was apparently surrounded by wildflowers, including orchids, with water that was so shallow and warm that babies could crawl through it. I shielded my eyes from the sun and looked towards the north, deciding that a walk was a damn fine idea—and might just be enough to get my writer's block flowing.

I was about to head off in that direction when a voice behind me made my heart skip. "Hello."

I froze. Due to the crashing waves I hadn't heard anyone coming, but instinctively I knew it must be him. I slowly turned and there was my neighbour, standing about four feet away from me. His right hand was shielding his eyes from the sun, but as I turned around he extended it out to me.

"I'm Jaime Batten. I live next door." He half turned to point to his cottage as he said this.

Like I hadn't noticed, I thought. I was suddenly aware that there was a good chance that I was looking like a mess. Given the breeze, I had clipped my hair up sloppily, and as a result, strands of untamed curls were blowing everywhere.

"I'm Ann. Ann Ralston," I said, finally finding my voice. "It's nice to meet you." I extended my right hand towards his and smiled. How could anyone not smile around this man?

He took my hand and shook it only slightly. In fact, he seemed to be holding it more than shaking it. Either way, the thought crossed my mind that he was holding on for a wee bit longer than what was typically customary, though I couldn't be sure if it was my imagination. His hand was warm and soft. He finally let go and moved beside me on the beach so that we were both out of the direct glare of the sun. Before I knew it, however, he was squatting on the beach, picking up an assortment of sticks and organic debris and tossing them on the nearby fire pit. He looked up at me and winked. At least I thought he winked.

"The waves bring in this junk sometimes, so every few days I try to stay on top of it. This is prime property up here." Now he smiled as he continued to pick up sticks for the fire and toss rocks onto a nearby rock pile. I felt weak at the knees. I couldn't help but stare at his legs. He was incredibly muscular and his faded jeans were pulled tight by his squat. He threw on a pair of aviator sunglasses and I noticed how his strong, clean hands worked like magic in the sand as they unearthed precious shells.

"So, um, how long have you had this cottage for?" I stammered, trying to do my best to keep up my side of the conversation.

"Oh, this place has been in my family for generations," he replied easily. As he said it, he looked at me intently.

"Really?" My eyes immediately went to the modern-looking, angular structure that was partially visible through the trees. "It doesn't look all that old."

"You're right," he responded. "I guess I should have said that the *property* has been in the family for generations. My parents took it over in the eighties, but about ten years after that the original building burned to the ground."

My hand went to my throat. "Really? That's horrible," I managed. "I hope nobody was hurt." I couldn't think of anything else to say.

Jaime's eyes shifted to the horizon. "Actually, people *were* hurt. My parents, in fact. They died in the fire."

"I'm so sorry," I murmured, my hand moving from my throat to cover my gasp. "How awful."

Jaime only nodded, his eyes still set on an invisible place far off in the distance. "Yeah, some kids were high on glue and they ended up torching various homes along this stretch of the beach." There seemed to be a long pause before he spoke again. "My parents were asleep and didn't have time to get out. I had no choice but to rebuild. I finished it a few years ago."

His sorrow penetrated me. I didn't know what to say. "You certainly did a beautiful job," I ventured, gesturing in the direction of his cottage. "I mean… I haven't really seen it, but it looks very nice from here. Unique. Like a chalet or something." *Oh my goodness, stop rambling, Ann!*

Jaime gave me one of his wonderful smiles. "Thanks. I've always sort of had a thing for architecture, so I thought I'd try something different. Something that would feel like a fresh start, you know?"

I could only nod.

"Mr. Barns lived in your little cottage, and by the grace of a miracle, Heart House was spared any torching by the kids. It's one of the only original cottages left on the beach, you know. I guess that's what makes it so… special."

My mind went back to the fact that Jaime had wanted to buy Heart House. Maybe that was why—for its nostalgia. Maybe it reminded him of good times with his parents before they were killed.

Suddenly he looked up at me and smiled. By golly, he was sucking the air out of me. "Nobody can figure out why they skipped over it. Some of the locals say it had to do with the hearts."

"The hearts," I repeated. *He knows about the hearts?*

"Didn't you notice all the little hearts inside your cottage? If I'm not mistaken, there's one on your front door, too."

I nodded. "Why are there so many?" I immediately felt silly that we were on this topic. Surely a grown man didn't want to discuss cute little hearts, of all things.

He winked. "Well, nobody's sure. But my theory is that they're meant to remind us to never let go of love." He bent down to pick up a flat rock. He tossed it into the water and I watched as it skipped four times. He turned to look at me. "Maybe it's meant to bring love to the people who live there." He smiled at me as he said this and I bit my lower lip. He threw another stick on the fire pit, took a step towards me, and removed his sunglasses. He looked directly into my eyes. His eyes were blue like the lake, and I felt like I'd drown in them at any second.

I think I may have gasped, but I wasn't entirely sure. I felt like I was on fire.

"Don't hesitate to let me know if I can help in any way. Mr. Barns was getting brittle in his old age, and I think some things were falling into disrepair towards the end." He looked towards my cottage as he spoke. "If you want me to fix the deck, let me know, okay?"

What's wrong with the deck? I silently questioned. I hadn't noticed anything that needed fixing.

"I better get going," he said. He smiled and his left hand took my arm in a very casual yet intimate way. "And nice to finally meet you, Ann."

I watched him as he walked back towards his cottage and could barely breathe. I felt like a meteor had crashed to the earth. I could have sworn that there was some sort of cosmic connection between us. It was almost as if he'd lit a spark when he'd touched me. My sister, with all of her new-age wisdom, would have said that he had given me a cosmic love tap, but was it really that? Maybe it was just static in the air. Could all those wind turbines have caused something funny to happen to the atmosphere? Was it even worth analyzing this whole scenario? I found myself shaking my head ay my own silliness. But as I sank into the sand, I was more than positive that something otherworldly had passed through us. It was unmistakable. And it scared me.

⁂

Later that evening, I found myself comfortably perched in a Muskoka chair on my deck trying to figure out what needed to be fixed as per Jaime's comments. As dusk set in my eyes scanned the perimeter, and although everything looked fine to me, it was useless to search out the flaws now. The air was brisk and necessitated a sweater, but the sound of the water lapping at the shores kept me outside. The wine from yesterday's episode had made my limbs lazy and my mind sloppy.

I couldn't stop thinking about Jaime. He was younger than me, and I knew I was only going to make life worse for myself if I even tried to imagine something happening between us. And for all I knew, he might already be in a relationship and was just being nice to his new neighbour. Certainly, there had been flirting. Was that so bad? I tried to get my mind back on track again.

The bottle was parked under my chair, and after pouring myself another glass and taking a long sip, I felt the wine course through my veins. I was definitely feeling relaxed as I stared towards his cottage. I tried to make out if there was any sort of view to his deck, and I couldn't help but hope to see him sitting out there admiring the same clear sky as I was. And yet I couldn't see a thing because of the dusk and the trees. *Unless none of his lights are on*, I thought in passing. My inhibitions were fleeting, and for a moment I even considered going over. But reality got the better of my plans when I stood and stumbled. I had consumed too much wine and was in no state to be carrying on any sort of interaction with this man. Clearly, it was time to go to bed. Alone.

It was pitch dark inside, and after bumping into the wall on my way up the stairs, I began laughing uncontrollably. I managed to remove all my clothing by the time I reached the top step and proceeded to open the windows so I could hear the water. My body continued to jar with unsteadiness, but I knew that the sound of the water would lull me to sleep in no time. The moon was full and cast a beautiful glow through the bedroom window as I eased myself into the heavenly bed. The duvet pulled away easily to allow for a quick retreat under its warmth, and my bare skin felt wonderful against the smooth cotton. I savoured the moment, feeling a terrible ache and desire as my body lay motionless in the dark. Could this be the source of my craziness with the man next door? That I was desperately in need of a man's touch? Or could I blame it on the wine?

I took a deep breath and rolled onto my stomach, writhing just enough to feel the friction of the sheets against my body, particularly against my breasts.

Every time the water crashed on the shore, my body chimed in unison. I rolled onto my back again and began to picture him. He was vivid in my mind, and so beautiful. I envisioned his face up close and I could see his gentle hands as they had looked when he'd explored the sand on our beach that afternoon.

In my mind I watched as he created mounds in the sand, moving his hands flawlessly to create perfect circles around and around until he found little pink shells in their centres. I watched as he played with the shells ever so carefully, precisely turning and caressing them with just the right amount of pressure to make them shine in the sunlight. They were becoming brighter as he played with them, and as the sun reflected off their surface, they burned with pleasure. Forceful streams of energy were sent to the surrounding sand, and channels writhing with electricity crept across a landscape of pure ecstasy.

My mind watched as his hands moved towards the water. There were more shells here, but they were slippery and wet. He needed to make them more beautiful, so he began polishing them, first with slow strokes, and then with increasing pressure and frequency. He buried his deft fingers deep within the sand, moving his hand back and forth. The shells intensified in light and beauty until they began to resemble diamonds from the fire that was being set within them. It was beginning to be too much, and his beautiful hands were moving quickly now because time was running out. A storm was coming and the shells were about to be washed away to sea. The waves were crashing onto the shore too quickly, and were rushing—rushing until all the shells were sucked into the depths of the lake as the water rushed in.

There was a moment of hesitation, then silence until the beach finally gave way to the calm after the storm.

CHAPTER 11

When the Canadian Thanksgiving weekend arrived in mid-October, I found myself tolerating another long three-hour drive to the cottage. I came to the realization that I wouldn't have enjoyed this trek every five days if it weren't for the desire to see a very special someone every weekend. Mondays had become the epitome of depression, and by Thursday, the twenty-four hour countdown would become unbearable for me. So when Thanksgiving Friday arrived, I was as joyful as ever.

The clocks had been changed the weekend prior and darkness had already set in when I finally pulled into Heart House's driveway. It was only after closing my trunk that I began to hear faint noises coming from the beach. I envisioned dog walkers along the shoreline as I stood very still and listened, but the noises did not waver. They were clearly coming from a fixed location on the beach. As I stood and listened, words and sounds became more audible and seemed to be coming from my back deck. Worse still, there seemed to be a fiery glow coming from that direction as well.

Panic ensued as I thought about the local kids and the torching scene that Jaime had told me about. I quietly entered my cottage and, without turning on the lights, I slowly crept towards the nearest back window.

My heart was racing for fear of what I would find, and yet as I peered through the kitchen window all I could see was a bonfire burning on the beach. My deck was dark and empty. I couldn't figure out who the heck was burning wood on my property at this time of year. Renee had said that people might easily walk across my beach, but did that mean they might pick a spot to light a fire, too?

There was another bout of laughter and women's voices. After surveying the area, I realized that it was the same bonfire pit where Jaime had been piling debris the other weekend. Was he having a bonfire? Did he have guests over? What the heck was going on?

I kept my lights off and moved to the French doors to get a better view. I still couldn't see everything, and it was killing me not to know what was going on. *Way to go, Ann,* I chided myself. *You're turning into an idiot stalker again.* With that thought, I immediately began turning on the lamps and lighting a few candles in the living room. It was then that my eye went to several stones arranged neatly on the sofa table. I hadn't noticed before, but they were all shaped like hearts. I recalled Renee's voice. *Little hearts everywhere.*

A warm glow began to fill the space, and as I took a moment to savour the usual cedar scent, I was jolted from my senses by a female scream erupting from the beach. This was immediately followed by an uproar of male laughter. My legs were unsteady as they carried me straight to the kitchen to uncork some wine. The playful scream had unnerved me, and although I tried to ignore it, my curiosity was piqued as I wondered who the females were. Did Jaime have a girlfriend—and could I bear to find out? Was she the one who had screamed? Maybe he'd grabbed her and tickled her…

Ignore it, Ann. I unpacked a box filled with food and morosely stared at the Thai dish that I had purchased in Toronto before I left. Everything had gone soggy and, despite the thought of rewarming it, I could see that it was not going to be a pleasant meal. Just at that moment, another scream erupted—more like a squeal, actually—and I bit my lower lip.

I was becoming edgy. It was then that my curiosity got the better of me, as did that one glass of wine on an empty stomach, because with a touch of spontaneous courage, I decided to head outside to spy. Never mind the rational side of myself that told me to mind my own business and put on my pyjamas instead. *Phooey.*

I opened the doors to the back deck and quietly stepped outside, completely conscious of the fact that I was tempting fate—and possible disappointment. The sound was carrying clearly now, and as far as I was concerned, it wouldn't hurt to cast a few furtive glances towards the fire to try to see as much as possible.

Sweetie, you need to let it go sometimes. Why do you do this to yourself? You are your own worst enemy. My mother's voice suddenly popped into my head. Okay, so she was probably right. But I needed her to be quiet. I bent down to strategically hide behind an overflowing planter of dead ivy as I strained my eyes for a better view. I was setting my wine glass beside me and making a mental note not to knock it over when I caught sight of Jaime sitting on a log.

His profile was suddenly clear in the light of the fire. He held a long stick and was stoking the fire, and the glow from the flames outlined his features perfectly. Though he was as handsome as ever, my eyes immediately zeroed in on the very pretty girl sitting next to him. She was about thirty—of course, younger than me—and definitely having the time of her life. They were all laughing at something and she kept placing her hand on Jaime's leg. I noticed that he didn't necessarily return the contact, which gave me some degree of hope. But still, the whole scene was essentially tearing me up inside.

And then, in a split second, he was looking up towards my cottage. I froze. *God help me—could he possibly have seen me?* I trembled. There was nothing like being a pathetic old woman who spies on her neighbours. For a second time.

I crouched down even further and moved towards my cottage, kicking over my wine glass in the process. *Dammit*, I cursed, then focused my energy on praying that the combination of darkness, trees, and ivy had obstructed his view. And then the dreadful moment came. He continued to stare, and then slowly got up and started walking towards my cottage.

I was excited and embarrassed at the same time. I couldn't quite figure out if he would be glad to see me and would welcome me to the fire, or if he was going to tell me to piss off and get a life. The agony was killing me, but I just couldn't seem to pull myself together enough to return to the house.

I heard him open the gate adjacent to the patio and in an instant he was standing at the bottom of the concrete steps to the left of my deck. "Ann? Oh, there you are. I saw your lights go on."

As I slowly rose to my feet, my mind began frantically searching for an excuse as to why I was crouching on my deck in the middle of the night. All of a sudden my head hit something hard and I felt an incredible surge of pain that was so intense I thought I was going to die right there and then. "Oh, Christ," I muttered to myself. Damn that wine.

"Ouch! Are you okay?" Jaime said, wincing. "That was quite the hit."

No, I was not okay. I'd just been caught spying on a man I was nuts about, and on top of that, he had to witness my klutziest moment of the year. I was mortified. I looked up to identify the culprit and saw that I'd been knocked senseless by a loose beam on the deck rail. *Pull it together*, Ann.

"I hope you'll let me fix that," Jaime offered, pointing to the railing. "What were you doing down there, anyways?"

So that's the repair he'd been referring to the other weekend on the beach. I reached up to feel for a bump while I surveyed the broken wine glass scattered across my deck. "I was just trying to…" I trailed off, searching for any plausible excuse. "To clean up some broken glass on my deck."

His eyes dropped to the scattered shards. "Here, let me help you. I wouldn't want you to hurt yourself," he offered, taking a step towards me.

"No, no, it's fine. I can do it tomorrow when there's better light." I turned my attention to rubbing my head because it was killing me.

"Well, if you're sure." He paused for a second and looked towards the bonfire before continuing. "I have some friends over and we're sitting down there by the fire, talking and having some drinks. Do you want to join us?" He gestured towards the beach before he shuffled his feet in the leaves.

Does he look a little nervous? I wondered. *Or is my mind playing tricks on me again?* I didn't know what to do or say. I desperately wanted to be around him, but not necessarily around those strange people that he called his friends. And yet, perhaps it would be safer to get to know him in a group. That way I wouldn't have to try to carry on one half of an intelligent conversation—which I didn't seem capable of doing around him. *Besides, you need to let loose*, I coaxed myself. *Quit worrying all the time and live a little. Grandma Lily worried her whole life and look where that got her. Dead at sixty.*

"Sure. Um… Just let me grab some wine and a sweater," I said.

"No need." He raised his voice just slightly as he spoke. He extended his hand towards me, and if he had been wearing white gloves he could have easily been mistaken for Prince Charming. He placed his hand on my gate and it eased open with a small creaking sound. "I have plenty of wine to share, and it's really quite warm by the fire. I'm sure you'll be fine, and if not…" He tilted his head ever so slightly and winked at me. "We'll figure out a way to keep you warm."

Zing. It was the only intelligible word I could think of at that moment.

CHAPTER 12

The bonfire soiree turned out to be quite pleasant. Jaime had four friends over, two of which were female, though I was relieved to discover that neither was an official girlfriend. However, I gathered that one—the touchy-feely one—was extremely fond of him. And although she aptly conveyed her desire as the night progressed, Jaime remained indifferent. He didn't join in with the flirt dance and actually seemed oblivious to it. I surmised that he probably got similar female attention all the time—and was therefore immune to it.

As the night progressed in front of the warm flames the group recalled many adventures from their school days. I wasn't sure if they had grown up on the lake or in another city. I didn't ask. Jaime, seemingly aware that I had little to add to these topics of conversation, threw glowing smiles in my direction every once in a while. He had a wonderful way of making me feel very welcome in his little circle. I learned quite a bit about my new neighbour that night. Jaime's parents were described as being extremely caring and deeply respected by the other four individuals, who seemed to have known Jaime from childhood. He had one older sister, who had died at the age of eighteen in a car accident. Apparently this was brought on by a combination of alcohol and speeding after a dance at their local high school. Her name was Louise, and all of the friends who had been riding in the car with her had survived. It was a tragic loss, and Jaime had been close to her.

He had entered into a career in policing almost ten years before and had quickly advanced through the ranks. He was extremely well respected and was now a private detective, often completing undercover work in various stages and disguises. He was thirty-four years old.

I was going to be forty-one, and although there was a span of more than six years between us, the age difference was not as bad as I had originally thought. And I was somewhat gratified when even the sleazy girl at the bonfire remarked that I looked fantastic—her choice of words—when I reluctantly revealed my age. I stole a glance towards Jaime as I mentioned it because I desperately wanted to gage his reaction, but he only smiled and took a swig from his beer, his eyes never leaving the fire.

I learned that his cottage was his home for the most part. He could be away for extended periods of time while on duty, but home was home and this was it. I also learned that he travelled extensively across North America and even internationally depending on the situation. I didn't want to imagine him being away for so long and wondered if it was worth asking what could possibly demand his attention for that length of time.

He seemed to be involved in serious undercover work
which made me think of espionage, but I decided to
mind my own business and save the question for later.

At one point, when the showgirl Amanda was
obviously under the influence of far too much alcohol,
she began to rub his back. He quickly got up and poked
at the fire. I sensed that he was uncomfortable, and I
was hoping that he would choose to sit back down
closer to me. Unfortunately, this didn't happen. He
ended up sitting on the lap of one of his male friends,
partially in jest, and when the entire lawn chair
collapsed under the weight, both men indulged in a fit
of laughter that seemed to go on for an eternity. I
couldn't help but smile at his playfulness. *When was the
last time I actually played?* I wondered, a brief wave of
sadness lapping at the back of my mind.

While Amanda continued to do her best to
communicate to Jaime her overt interest, the other
female in the group, Siobhan, was fast putting me at ill
ease. She had a terrible habit of staring, and I grew
more and more uncomfortable under her speculative
gaze. She seemed very intuitive, almost as if she could
read every thought that was coursing through my skull.
She was of Irish descent, and although she had a rough
edge to her, she was actually quite pretty in a non-
descript way. Her blunt black hair and piercing blue
eyes created an aura of distance, but the features on her
face were jarring in some way. Maybe it was
asymmetry, but I couldn't figure it out. I was envious of

her slick hair as I continually pulled my unruly sandy blonde curls away from my face.

When it was getting late, Jaime suggested that it was time to butt the fire. I was sad to see the evening end, despite the fatigue that was setting in. But it was definitely into the wee hours of the morning, and I knew my wonderful bed was calling. Amanda had fallen asleep on Siobhan's shoulder, and I smiled as Siobhan roughly poked her so they could walk back to the cottage together and retire for the night. Perhaps they were colleagues or even best friends, but for the life of me, I could not figure out how that combination of friends could possibly be. They seemed so different, and yet there was an undeniable affection between the two. Suddenly I was swept with a wave of longing to spend some time with Renee. I made a mental note to have her and the girls up to Heart House soon.

The four friends headed back towards Jaime's cottage and I was left alone with him at the fire. I watched as he kicked sand into the pit to extinguish the glowing coals.

"Thanks for inviting me. I had a good time." I paused and looked at the ground, kicking some sand with my feet before looking up at him again. It was difficult to talk to him and make eye contact at the same time. There was suddenly a distinct discomfort between the two of us that couldn't be explained, and I was positive it wasn't originating entirely from me. The awkwardness hung in the air and seemed to trap the two of us in a twisted time warp. I had to break the silence. "It was a hot fire," I said, and as soon as the words were out of my mouth I wanted to roll my eyes. *Way to state the obvious, Ann.*

"With winter approaching, I think it'll be the last one of the season." He threw the long branch he'd been using as a poker on top of the smoking fire pit and turned to look at me.

I quickly looked away, oppressed by the discomfort between us. I began shivering and could feel the cold air stinging. My hands hugged my body and rubbed my upper arms to retain some small amount of warmth.

"Hopefully I'll see you again soon. Sleep well," he said. And that was it. Just like that. After speaking those words he seemed to leap like a panther onto the mysterious path that existed between our cottages, and was gone in a flash.

I suddenly found myself alone on the beach, shivering uncontrollably—and this time I wasn't sure if it was from the cold or not. The path to my cottage was illuminated by the full moon, and I was suddenly as charged as a lighthouse beacon overlooking Lake Superior. My emotions lit on fire, and I couldn't think straight. Confusion and frustration bled into longing and desire. I felt like I had no control over myself, and something in the universe was making me crazy. I was dizzy with wants and desires, and I couldn't make heads or tails of anything. And, worst of all, I couldn't understand him. In some ways I felt like I was no closer to knowing him than I'd been last weekend. He was driving me mad—and this was not good.

After making it to my cottage I crawled under my thick duvet. I added the quilt for extra warmth and did by best to sink into the comfortable oblivion of the bed. But this time, sleep was not coming. I stared at my bedside clock in a daze, watching the minutes slowly pass. I recall the time of 4:25 a.m. before I must have fallen asleep, only to awake the next morning with a disastrous, hideous black mood foaming at the edge of my consciousness. That, and one big giant headache.

I drove home to Toronto a day early and felt rage surging through my blood. For the life of me, I really couldn't explain any of it.

CHAPTER 13

The long and lonely stretch of highway leading from the cottage to the city provided me with some much-needed time to think. In the midst of a torrential downpour, I decided that it was necessary to try to get Jaime out of my head. I actually felt like he was becoming a slow-growing tumour embedded deep within the sulci of my brain matter, and he was beginning to take control over my cognitive and motor functioning. Not to mention he was also affecting my sympathetic nervous system in a profound way.

I tried to tell myself that my feelings about this man were merely something I'd created—some unfounded fantasy that I'd dreamed up to infuse drama and emotion into my otherwise dull existence. After all, I was a divorced research assistant at a forgettable consulting firm. I knew that whatever I was feeling about Jaime was most likely a romantic fairy tale that was going nowhere, and yet at the same time it gave me hope. My rational self was telling me that he was too young for me, and that I was mistaking his courtesy for flirting. *He was only being polite, Ann*, I told myself. *Inviting you to the bonfire was the neighbourly thing to do. What else were you expecting?* Had I thought that he would profess his undying love for me and take me

right there on the sand? I groaned. I was clearly
deluded.

But my mind kept inching back to the
possibility that maybe there truly was something there.
But it could never work. My mind jumped ahead,
rationalizing a situation that likely didn't even deserve a
second thought. *He's too young for me. Plus, he's too
busy.* His job took him far away, and for long stretches
of time. Even if there was a chance that he was
interested, it was clearly a no-win situation— and just
when I was at a time in my life when I needed
composure.

What was it about him that shattered my sense
of equilibrium so utterly? Surely to goodness I had
encountered handsome men in my lifetime before. Why
did this one have to spin me in circles? *Forget him,
Ann,* said my mother's voice. But why would the
universe put us together unless there was a reason for
it? Maybe I was experiencing this chaos for a reason;
maybe there was some cosmic force that was pulling
me towards him.

*There are no coincidences in life, Ann. Things
happen for a very particular reason—a reason that is
related to your destiny. This could be synchronicity.*

Thank you, Thea.

Synchronicity. Every part of me tried to make
sense of this. His lingering touches, his gaze, his
attempts to include me, his winks and his smiles and his
words. But how could I explain the way that he could

simultaneously distance himself from me? Every part of this situation was a dichotomy.

As I began to pass through the suburbs, I suddenly wondered whether he realized that he was torturing me. Perhaps he was aware of his effect on me, and given the naïve person that I was, he found it compelling to watch me fall for it. He must have known that he had been born with beautiful genes, and perhaps he'd mastered his craft so well that he'd left a string of broken hearts along the way. What if I was just another victim of his hook, line, and sinker tactic? I had always thought of myself as someone who was immune to those sorts of games, but now that I was caught in the middle of this web, I was beginning to feel ashamed by my lack of insight.

The rain finally subsided when I entered the city, and as my windshield wipers slowed to half tempo I became mesmerized by a couple standing at a nearby bus stop. My car pulled to a stop at a red light and I found myself staring at them. He was saying something to her and he looked irritated. Interestingly, her face held a distinctly vacant look. She only stared ahead, not saying a word as he kept talking. He seemed to be barking some type of order at her, or maybe he was lecturing her about something. She had a terrible faraway look to her eyes that was entirely revealing—but not to him.

My mind raced to my year married to Randy, and to the profound loneliness that had marked those isolated months. And then the light turned green and a car honked behind me.

CHAPTER 14

For the next six months, I went to the cottage only sporadically. The long drive was becoming difficult in the bad winter weather, and the shoreline's charm lay dormant as it turned steely and gray. I quickly discovered why so many summer houses were boarded up and deserted along Lake Huron. It was the wind.

Stepping outside my cottage, it tore through even the heaviest of woolen jackets, chilling me to the bone. It would fly off Lake Huron like an evil force and wreak havoc on anyone who dared to confront it. Its harsh whistling sounds did nothing for my psyche, and I longed for the gentle sounds of the water that I'd heard late last summer. Furthermore, Jaime had been away for work since late fall. And as a result, I was miserable at Heart House, and not even this misery could spur on my writing.

So when March finally arrived, I tried to bolster my emotions knowing that spring was just around the corner. I scheduled an all-out girls' weekend for late March and held onto a faint hope that Jaime might have returned by then.

The weather for the girls' weekend was shaping up to be clear and mild, and the snow was finally retreating. As I neared Lake Huron on my long Friday drive, I realized that I hadn't felt this excited to be on the way to Heart House since Thanksgiving. I passed the wind turbines and my heart began to beat noticeably faster. I couldn't wait to get to the McKellars' store. Fran and I had become very good acquaintances over a succession of spontaneous visits, and I was curious to find out if she had any new information about Jaime.

"My Lord! Ann, where have you been?"

Fran was tickled pink to see me as I passed under the chimes on the old store's front door. She gave me a great big hug—one that made me feel wonderfully good and fuzzy inside. I thought about her hugging Jaime in the same way and wondered whether it felt different for her.

"I brought you a little something, Fran," I said. I held out a paper bag to her.

"Oh my word, Ann, that's not what I think it is, is it?" she asked me, her nose already twitching. She peered inside the bag at the French pastries and made an elaborate face. "It is!"

"It's *pain au chocolate* you like, right?" I asked, remembering a conversation we'd had months ago.

"Right on, kiddo! Oh, you're such a sweet girl. Now tell me all about your exciting big city life. We've missed you, you know."

I began to tell her about my busy week in the city and about the upcoming weekend as I filled a wicker basket with an array of veggies, bread, and dips. Fran followed me around the store, listening intently and clucking her tongue. As I mused over the red onion display, she quickly exchanged the bulb of garlic in my basket for another, explaining that the ones at the bottom of the display were fresher. "Mr. McKellar likes to get rid of the old ones first, so always dig deep. He has a way with how he sorts these things."

I smiled and held my shopping basket close to my chest as I watched how she deftly rearranged the balsamic vinegars. "Ann, I hope you don't mind me asking, but are you with anyone right now? I mean, Bob and I have been seeing you come up here on and off for the past six months, and you're always alone."

I must have looked uncomfortable, because she abandoned the vinegars and lay a motherly hand on my arm.

"Trust me, kiddo, I know this is really none of my business. But you're a pretty girl. I mean, Bob never stops telling everyone about what a good looking girl you are, and it's just that you are so sweet and nice and always wanting to do such lovely things for everyone." She gestured to my basket. "Like this party you're putting on for your friends."

There was a terrible silence that lasted far too long, but I finally managed to smile at Fran. She was breaking my heart. I wasn't sure if this conversation was heading towards a lecture, or if she was simply being nosy.

She patted my arm. Before she said anything, I knew what was coming. And when it did, it was like a serpent's tongue—smooth, slick, and dangerous. "What about Jaime? The two of you must have become acquainted by now, haven't you?"

I paused and put down my basket. My heart began to beat rapidly, and I felt my cheeks flush. "Mrs. McKellar…" Now it was my turn to pat her arm. "Jaime seems like a wonderful person, but to be honest, I barely know him. We've only met a couple of times. He hasn't been at the cottage for the last few months, which is strange because he always seemed to be there in the summer, and now he's just… gone. What do you think may have happened?"

I knew darned well that he must be away for work, but I waited and wondered if she was going to take the bait. I smiled again but she refused to make eye contact with me, and instead began to fiddle with one of the signs displaying artichokes. "Oh, well, Jaime just gets very busy with work sometimes. You must know that he works in law enforcement? Well, that job takes him away quite a bit. This spring, for instance, he's had to travel to Colorado—I know that much, but I don't know the details. But Bob said it's one that might end up in the papers."

She stopped fiddling with the signs and turned to look at me. Her face was very serious and she appeared to be reading something that was clearly evident on my face. And then the realization dawned on me that she was one step ahead of me. She knew exactly what I had been fishing for the entire time. I felt my face turning red.

I looked at my watch. "Gosh, I really need to get going, Mrs. McKellar. I lost track of time, and my friends are going to be arriving soon!"

Fran gave me an appeasing smile that told me plainly that she wasn't buying it. Still, she played along and packed up my groceries as quickly as she could. As I was leaving I heard her call, "We don't know when he'll return, Ann. Otherwise, you know I would have told you. But it could be any day now."

I nearly tripped down the three steps leading to my car. I jammed the key in the ignition and felt like one big fool.

***

There were five of us, including myself, and we were enjoying ourselves immensely. The case of wine sat squarely on the kitchen floor, and we were on bottle number three. The fire was going strong, and we were scattered about, eating to our hearts' content. Everyone had brought food and the meal was the equivalent of a royal buffet. I was stuffed to the bone and plumping some pillows behind me when Renee decided to intrude upon my evolving state of relaxation.

"Where's the hot babe, Annie?" She spoke with a Texan drawl and I realized that she was more than just drunk. Too thin, I thought. She needed more meat on her bones to prevent her from getting intoxicated so quickly.

My friend Janet sat down next to me. "Yeah, Ann, I hear this guy is one hot super-looking boy… and he lives next door? What's his deal? Is he married?"

Oh, for God's sake. I decided to pour myself another glass of wine and spilled some in the process. I began blotting the mess with some napkins. "He's not married, and to tell you the truth, I really don't know much about him. I've only met him twice. He's a detective. Actually, he's on a job right now—possibly in the United States."

Renee's words slurred. "Give Mr. Jaime a call. He could be next door as we speak—you never know. Maybe I should go and check…" She was sitting on the rug in front of the fireplace, leaning against the couch. She stretched out, sliding her long bare legs against one another. The thought of Renee going over there in a drunken stupor immediately sobered me up.

Gloria, my trusted mind reader and a friend for life, grabbed my hand. Pulling me towards her, I heard her whisper, "She's going to be fine. Don't worry, I'll watch her. She's all talk. Relax, okay?"

I leaned back against the plush pillows of the couch and realized for the first time that the wrought-iron knobs on the hutch were actually little hearts. I blinked and then looked across at Gloria, whom I deeply admired. She was one person who'd survived everything that could possibly go wrong in her life, and yet she still managed to see a half-full cup.

Our other friend, Lori, immediately spoke up. "The guy next door—is his name Jaime *Batten*, by any chance? My brother knows a detective, and his name is Jaime Batten. I have no idea why I remember useless information like that, but I do."

Now this sparked my attention, because Lori's brother was an officer. I vaguely recalled Jaime telling me his name the first time we met on the beach, and indeed he had said Batten. Why did I feel that there were six degrees of separation going on here?

"How would your brother know him?" It was Renee's turn to ask questions. She seemed to regain some composure as she sat upright and laid a blanket across her legs.

"Well, if it's the same guy—and I don't really know that for sure—then I'm pretty sure he picked my brother up once when they were all heading to some event. Does he drive a sporty BMW?"

I sipped my wine more slowly. "Yes, something like that," I said with caution, thinking back to the car I had seen parked in his driveway.

"And?" Renee prompted Lori. For once I was glad for her incessant probing.

"Well, he looked like a model out of New York, from what I can recall. My brother called him the pretty boy, but said he's sharp as a chisel and that you most certainly would not want to get on his bad side."

I groaned, thinking back on the real estate deal. *I sure hope I'm not on his bad side without knowing it*, I thought.

"Well then, we must be talking about the same pretty boy," concluded Renee.

"Small world," said Lori, reading my thoughts exactly. She turned to me. "If you're not interested in him, Ann, I may have to take a closer look next time he comes around." She winked at me and I could see that she was joking. Then she added, "Although I'm pretty sure my brother said there was something weird about him with respect to women."

"Yeah, like he makes them swoon!" slurred Renee, decidedly drunk again. "Annie! You need to move in on that!"

I stuffed a few slices of havarti in my mouth and promptly headed for the kitchen. I realized that I might be better off watching my cheese intake from here on in.

Summer was coming and who knew when Jaime Batten might be back.

CHAPTER 15

There was something about the arrival of the month of May that evoked good feelings in me. Whether it was the scent of lilacs or the chirping of the robins that skittered in the rain, it was a time that seemed to promise renewal and optimism. It somehow gave me the much-needed courage to ask my boss for a week to work offsite at the cottage.

"You know, Ann, I'm quite aware that the long weekend is coming up."

Frank Ellis was a perfectionist, and he had a way of saying things that made me feel guilty before I'd even committed a crime. He was sitting at his black desk, which was too large in my opinion, and staring angrily at his computer screen. He moved his glasses to the tip of his nose and seemed perplexed by something he was reading. As usual he barely made eye contact, which was something that I'd gotten used to years ago.

"Can you give me absolute assurance that this project will be completed by the following Tuesday?" He was referring to our research proposal on plastic toxins, namely bisphenol A and a possible link to various prenatal conditions. I couldn't help but notice how his long, slender fingers were tracing the deeply ingrained lines on his forehead as he spoke. "As you know, the grant submission is due on Wednesday, which will only give me one day to review it." He finally broke the connection with his computer and looked up at me. He was losing his hair at a rapid rate and a few strands were completely out of place.

As if these deadlines haven't been weighing on my shoulders for weeks, I thought grouchily, but I said nothing.

"If you want a week away from this place—and still be paid—you'll need to ensure that your work is exceptional," Frank continued. "I don't want to be wasting my time next Tuesday." He pushed his glasses back into place and carefully sorted some papers in front of him.

I sighed. I knew that this man was fond of me—he perhaps even considered me a friend, albeit a subordinate one—but he could be infuriatingly remote at times. I shifted ever so slightly on my feet and cleared my throat before I spoke. "You won't have to waste any time. Rest assured."

As I walked out of his office, I laughed—quietly, of course—because I knew I could finish the rest of the project in three days, not five, if I could only keep my head on my shoulders at the cottage.

I couldn't help but wonder if Jaime would be there to celebrate the Victoria Day long weekend. He had been gone since October and I had a hard time trying to imagine what kind of assignment had kept him away for this long. Sometimes I would picture him in some drug-infested haven bringing down mafia hitmen and dragging the entire cartel to the Supreme Court of Canada. Then my mind would wallow in disturbingly low places as I'd envision him, bearded, in a room with beaded curtains doing hard drugs himself with barely-dressed women hanging off him. The whole image became so disgustingly ugly in my mind that I would have to stop because, like usual, I was obsessing. Clearly, I had to stop thinking of him.

As it turned out, when I arrived at Heart House there was still no sign of his car. A deflated feeling came over me, and yet it was probably for the best, given the work I had to do. The mere thought of Frank was enough to get me going, and although I managed to get about three quarters of the work done by Wednesday, the sun decided to peek out on Thursday and create havoc with my motivation. My deck was calling and I couldn't resist.

I had opened the French doors earlier so that I could hear the water, and as I stepped outside, the warm wind embraced me. I could almost feel the melanin activating under my skin, and it was the most blessed feeling in the whole world. The water was more turbulent than usual, and quite murky—a definite sign of transition as the lake prepared for the start of summer. I scanned the horizon, and then slowly turned my eyes south, towards his house. I was damn curious.

Not once had I dared to venture over there. But now here I was, and as virtually no one was around—

especially not him—it was a perfect time to go snooping. Like clockwork, my mother's voice popped into my head. *What other people do is not your business, dear. That's one of the best pieces of advice I could give you.* I shrugged off the voice and, within seconds of the passing thought, I was prancing off my deck like a ballerina in the wind. The trees had become full with spring foliage, and I realized I had missed the privacy they created. The branches were overgrown and in need of a good pruning, but I was able to find a distinct, well-worn footpath that made me think that Jaime and Mr. Barns had more in common than I had originally thought.

I then stopped short. Directly in front of me was an aged pine, carved deeply with the initials JB and MS. There was a misshapen heart surrounding the letters. The identity of JB was obvious to me: Jaime Batten. But who was MS? Confusion set in, and there was a terrible sinking feeling in my stomach.

I told myself to move along, which thankfully I did despite my heart drumming rapidly. It was evident that I was nearing his property and I felt like a complete idiot. I was stalking a person who was virtually a stranger to me, not to mention that I was now trespassing. The question of whether to turn around entered my mind, but my she-devil ego urged me on.

What if someone sees me? How will I ever explain what I'm doing here? I figured I could always say that I was delivering the mail. And yet, I wasn't carrying any mail. *Shit. I should have brought something over to be on the safe side.* I shook my head and nearly laughed out loud to myself. *Let's be mature about this, Ann. I'm not twelve years old, for God's sake. I'll just say that I was dropping by to see if he was home.*

My arms moved like a swimmer's as I cleared low-hanging boughs away in every direction. In a few more moments an opening finally came into view, and then I was standing on soft sand and tall grass, staring at his incredible cottage. To say I was stunned would be an understatement. I'd seen the occasional angle and peak through the trees from the beach, but the building was much more spectacular up close than I had ever imagined. The structure he'd built resembled a modern piece of art. It appeared to be two storeys, but there were so many angles and sections to his cottage that there could be at least three or four levels in there. Cedar shingles made up the roof, and a creamy yellow hue graced the clapboard. Then there were the windows; they were everywhere! *Good Lord, this is right out of Architectural Digest.*

I walked towards his multi-level deck, which was at least three times the size of mine. He had exquisite patio furniture and a built-in stone barbeque on one level, and the other level housed beautiful cream-coloured Muskoka chairs for lounging. They were identical to the chairs I'd come across on the beach last fall, halfway between our properties. *So I guess that solves one mystery—those chairs are his.* There were overflowing potted plants everywhere, complete with an array of beautiful colours and textures. *Who on earth planted these flowers?* I wondered with a renewed twinge of jealousy, for their tastefulness had the air of a woman's touch. The surrounding landscaping was equally fabulous. *How did he pay for this?* I wondered.

My eyes darted to an oversized wicker chaise lounge built for two. The cushions were enormous and plump and I couldn't resist the thought of lying on it one night—with Jaime. I debated about going any closer to his house. Though I felt the extreme urge to peek through his windows, my sensible mind was telling me to move on and get back to work. *See, mom? I do have at least* some *sense.*

Before I left, I turned to look at his view of the shoreline. The water was incredible, as usual, and somehow looked even more enticing from this vantage point. A warm breeze blew past me and I could completely understand why he lived here all year long. In fact, the only question that remained in my mind was, How did he pull himself away at all? It was a magical place; I felt like I was finding oil in my own backyard.

"Ma'am?"

I must have jumped at least two feet in the air, and I know that I screamed. I half turned to see who was behind me.

"Goodness, I'm so sorry. I didn't mean to startle you."

It took me a moment to compose myself, as I was certain I was having a full-blown heart attack at that very moment.

"Are you a girlfriend of Jaime's?"

Yes, sir, I wish, I thought as I tried to calm my breathing. My heart rate was at least one eighty. "No, I'm not. I'm his neighbour. Ann Ralston." I spoke in a breathy way as I held out my jittery hand.

"Nice to meet you, Ann. I'm Jim Lafferty."

"Are you a friend of Jaime's?" I asked.

"Yeah, I am. Do you know if he's around?"

I raised my sunglasses to the top of my head to buy myself some time. "He's uh… not here right now." I half smiled and decided to throw out a little white lie. "That's actually why I'm here. I check on the place from time to time to make sure things are… you know… alright."

Good God, Ann. Checking in on the place? Where did that come from? Like Jaime would ever ask me to do that. I could swear Jim was looking at me strangely now. "You know," I said as I looked towards Jaime's beautiful potted plants. "I water the plants if they need it, and… and check to see if there's any junk mail." I gestured towards the house with a twirling index finger and shifted my weight uncomfortably. *Sink yourself deeper, baby.*

Jim paused for a few seconds and scrutinized me. Then his face erupted into a beautiful bold smile. I couldn't be sure what he was thinking, but there was a darn good chance that he was seeing right through me and knew I was a container of lies.

"Of course," he remarked. "Now I remember… Jaime did tell me about the pretty girl who moved in next door. In fact, he asked me to say hello if I ran into you." My heart rate was immediately up again. I was having a fight or flight reaction. Jaime had mentioned me to this guy?

I couldn't speak, and Jim looked concerned for a moment. His smile vanished as he kept speaking, probably with the intention of putting me at ease. "I met Jaime through my wife. She works at the same hospital where Jaime's stepmother worked before she died."

Stepmother? I wondered. There had been no mention of a stepmother at the bonfire last fall.

"My wife's the one who does all his gardening," he offered, gesturing towards the potted plants. Then he glanced at his watch. "I was just swinging by to check up on things myself."

I groaned. Jaime had probably asked Jim to look in on his house, which blew my cover story out of the water. "I was just heading back to my place," I stammered, pointing in the general direction of Heart House.

"Don't you need to check on things inside?" he asked, and I swore I saw a glint in his eyes as he spoke.

"Well, c'mon, I've got a key." He turned to walk towards the house. "By golly, he's been gone what... at least six months?" Jim asked, making small talk.

"Eight," I said under my breath as we ascended another set of stairs to reach his back doors.

Jim opened the locks and we were in. I wondered if Jaime had installed the same French doors at my cottage, as they looked remarkably similar. There was a sweet smell to the house as we made our way into his kitchen, which overlooked his deck and the shoreline. There was an abundance of light streaming in everywhere. The great room to the left had a towering stone fireplace that dwarfed the one at Heart House. I stood at the kitchen island and slowly ran my hand across the cool, black granite countertops. My eyes were drawn upwards; the place was literally consumed by wooden beams and stonework. It was magnificent, and my little cottage paled in comparison. I immediately noticed that books were everywhere. He must have been a voracious reader. For some reason I hadn't expected that, and it made me realize just how much there was to Jaime Batten that I did not know.

"Everything look okay, Ann?" The corners of Jim's mouth were turned upwards in an ever so slight grin.

"Yes, I think so," I stammered, backing through the doorway and nearly falling down the deck stairs. Jim followed me out and locked up behind him.

"Well, it was nice to meet you, Ann. I'm glad to know that someone is keeping an eye on the place while Jaime's gone."

I could only nod and smile as I waved goodbye and headed back to the path that connected Jaime and me. I wondered if it really did.

CHAPTER 16

The remainder of Thursday passed uneventfully and was marred by thick rain clouds and torrents of rain, but by Friday morning my work was complete. I spent the afternoon in the garden, glad to get my hands dirty with something tangible for once. The tulips were happy, and I was happy to see the hosta sprouts befriending their columbine neighbours. A section of sprouting lilies took up the entire garden on the east side of the house, and I pondered moving them into direct sun.

Despite the monotony of pulling weeds, I found that the repetition in gardening created a self-regulatory effect that eased my mind of its worries. I could finally see why people found gardening pleasurable. As the shadows lengthened on Friday evening, I stood back and admired my progress. Yes, I truly did have a newfound love for gardening.

"Hey, Ann. How've you been?"

The hair on the back of my neck rose, yet I didn't jump out of my skin this time. I turned to face him, and as my eyes met his gaze, I could see that he looked a little thinner. His cheeks seemed hollow and I found myself wondering what he could possibly have endured over the past eight months. And yet, the more I studied him, the more I could see that the contours of his face accentuated his beautiful features even more.

"I'm great, Jaime. How about you? You've been gone such a long time!" I said this with a stitch of irony in my voice; he had no idea how I had yearned for him each and every day of his absence. My nerves began to twitch, so I unconsciously crossed my arms in front of me as I shifted my weight, completely forgetting that my gloves were covered in wet soil. Bits and pieces of dirt smeared across my arms before falling to the ground. *Nice one, Ann.*

"Oh, God," I said. I looked down at the mess on my arms, stretching my hands out in front of me. "I was just gardening... as you can see." I tried to laugh it off, but my nervousness was no doubt fully transparent.

"You're doing a great job," he said, grinning and looking around. "Mr. Barns would be thrilled to know that you're taking care of his little garden."

I watched as he took a few strides towards my deck and sat down on the steps. His worn jeans were hugging his muscular legs, and his complexion had been darkened by the sun. I wondered if his assignment had taken him south, but then I remembered that Fran had said Colorado.

He was leaning forward and resting his elbows on his knees when he dropped his head and ran his hands through his hair. As he began to rub the back of his neck, I felt like I was going to start drooling.

"Tough few months?" I asked, as coherently as possible.

"Yeah," he sighed. "It was a difficult assignment and I'm definitely exhausted." He looked up at me and smiled. His eyes seemed brighter than they had in the fall, but it could have been the reflection off the water. The contrast to his darker skin was incredible. "I'm glad to be home, though."

He leaned back on my step, stretched out, and crossed his legs in front of him. Every contour on the lower half of his body stood out and I tried not to stare. *God, he should be in a photo shoot*, I thought. I noticed a large scar that was at least six inches long traversing the underside of his forearm; it was strange how I hadn't noticed it before. He stared at me for a while and then looked out at the water. There was an awkward silence. Something seemed amiss, but I couldn't place it. I began to feel uncomfortable. Why couldn't I be at ease around this guy?

"Did anything exciting happen while I was gone?" He was staring at me intently now, raising his eyebrows questioningly. There was a curious yet mischievous look on his face.

I laughed out loud, and he immediately looked puzzled because he wasn't in on my apparent joke. "Yes, as a matter of fact. I celebrated one pretty wild weekend with a bunch of crazy women. You're lucky we didn't trespass over to your property and trash it."

He smiled in response and tilted his head to one side. "Hell, I missed the party? That's not fair, Ann." He winked at me and I took a deep breath.

"You sure did, mister." Now it was my turn to tease. For the life of me, I didn't know how I came to be so cocky when only a moment before I had been overcome with nerves and discomfort. And yet it happened uncontrollably, although my cheeks were on bloody fire. I bent down to pick up my spade because I desperately needed something to distract me.

Then he spoke again, but slower this time. "Well, isn't that ironic. I'm having a little party tonight and it would be nice if you came by."

Something twitched at the back of my neck, so I fiddled with the weeds in the bucket and stared at the cracks in the deck. I could feel his gaze penetrating me. There was another long pause.

"Some of the people you met at the bonfire will be there, and the rest are a friendly bunch that don't bite," he continued. "And I'll be there. Plus, if worse comes to worse and you absolutely hate it, you don't have far to go. It's just a hop, skip, and a jump to get home."

From my position crouched on the ground I could hear him stand up and walk towards me. He stopped right in front of me, then crouched down and carefully brushed some soil from my left cheek with his outstretched hand. We were facing each other and I could feel his breath on my skin. I thought I was going to collapse.

"It's casual," he went on, though his eyes seemed to be saying something completely different. "We'll start around seven or eight. There'll be lots of food, so don't stuff yourself ahead of time. Will you come?"

I needed to look elsewhere because he was so damn close, and making eye contact with him felt insanely dangerous. *Get it together, Ann.*

"Sure." It was all I could muster.

"Great. Then I guess I'll see you later." He stood up quickly, and as he brushed past me, I swore I could feel the sting of air between us.

I took a deep breath to calm myself while I collected my gardening tools from the cool ground. As I walked clumsily towards the shed at the front of the cottage, I began to feel extremely proud of myself for not looking back—and for not tripping.

***

Later that evening I began to develop a severe case of hyperactivity. If anyone were to have peered into my cottage, they would have seen a frantic idiot running from room to room, trying on different clothes, gaging the temperature, and standing in front of the mirror at least fifteen times. I jostled with the idea of wearing a favourite cotton blouse—one with dainty little straps and bare shoulders. It was a slinky number meant for hot summer nights, and although it was fairly warm for the season, there was a damn good chance that I would freeze as the evening progressed.

As I held the blouse against my skin and gazed into the mirror, a car horn blew and loud voices could be heard outside. A cascade of headlights hit my window like a spotlight, and after peering out I was able to count at least five cars at Jaime's house already. By no means was this going to be a small soiree. A small lump formed at the back of my throat, and within a split second the tiny blouse was on. To heck with it; cold or not, I was going to show some skin tonight.

I peered into the small mirror above my bathroom sink, assessing my face. My cheeks were still flushed from that afternoon, and in hopes of bringing out the same brazenness that had come over me in the garden, I opted to straighten my hair for a change.

The clock read seven o'clock but I didn't want to head over yet. My nerves were acting up so I poured myself a glass of wine and tried to envision what the night would be like. I had no idea what to expect, or what I would see, and the uncertainty did little to settle the butterflies in my stomach—so I poured myself another glass of wine instead. I figured that the only thing I could do was simply try to have a good time— and keep my wits about me.

Jaime's recent absence had made me realize that it was important for me to end the crazy infatuation I had with him. He hadn't really shown any clear signs of a mutual attraction, and yet he said and did things that seemed to have at least a slight sprinkling of it. He was unlike any other man I had met, and it was all so confusing. I desperately needed an opportunity to speak to him on a more personal level so that I could test out some theories. *Will tonight offer us that much-needed moment?* I rolled my eyes; I couldn't even picture myself saying anything beyond small talk. I poured another splash of wine.

When the clock neared the half past seven mark, I decided it was time to hold my head up high and make my way over. As I stepped out onto my deck to finish my third glass of wine, I could hear Colin James in the distance.

> *She moves like the wind got a fire in her eyes,*
> *Well, she can bring down rain from the clear blue skies,*
> *Make the sun go down with a wave of her hand,*
> *Well, she can make a King of an ordinary man,*
> *She's gonna make you dance, she's gonna make you sing,*
> *When she gives you some of that voodoo thing,*
> *Ooh, my voodoo thing...*

What an absolutely fitting song, I thought, swigging the last of my wine and carefully glancing at my reflection in the back window. All in check. I tried to locate the path that connected our cottages, but it was more difficult to find in the dark than I had anticipated. So, after my face was repeatedly struck with a slew of pine needles, I changed course and ventured towards Lake Road in order to approach Jaime's from the front. Given the recent rain, I figured that mud puddles were likely scattered in inconspicuous places in the bush anyways, and as far as I was concerned, there had been enough dirt on me for the day.

Wine on an empty stomach had me feeling fairly relaxed, so it was with ease that I opened his front door and walked right in as if it was my second home. The music seemed to come from every corner of the house, and Jaime's beautiful home was awash in warm candle light. There were many people, and they seemed to be everywhere. He certainly had quite a few acquaintances. I immediately recognized Siobhan by the fireplace, although her hair was much shorter than the last time I'd seen her at the bonfire. She cut me a quick, unfriendly glance and then looked away. I was immediately reminded that there was something about her that bothered me.

I moved towards the back of the house where the large living room seemed to blend into his huge kitchen. Food was laid out everywhere, which explained the many people milling about nearby. I couldn't help but notice a group of men who were most definitely gay. There were at least four of them. It was pretty obvious to me that they were homosexual, and I wondered if the two pretty girls chatting with them picked up on this. One of the men looked over and smiled at me in a welcoming way. I was curious about his connection with Jaime.

My rumbling stomach proved to be more important than any man or woman, because I was instantly distracted as I neared the spread on the table. Jaime must have had the party catered, because the dishes looked incredible. I stuffed something decorated with prosciutto and rosemary into my mouth and scanned for Jaime. He was nowhere in sight.

"Well, hello there. What would you like to drink?"

I turned to find a man standing at Jaime's island holding a bottle of white wine in one hand and a bottle of red in the other. He was rather handsome, but I could tell immediately that he knew it. He struck me as the type of man who played the field a lot.

With my mouth still partially full, I pointed to the red. "Red would be great, thanks," I mumbled. *Who is this guy?* I wondered. *He sure is mighty bold and friendly right off the bat. He doesn't seem like the type who'd be a friend of Jaime's.*

The mystery man grabbed a clean glass from the counter, and for a moment I wondered if he was one of the catering guys. But upon closer examination, I could see that he wasn't. He was wearing a regular white polo shirt with jeans, and his dark hair had a heavy dose of hair gel applied to it. He was definitely on the muscular side. He handed me a glass of red, and I admired Jaime's glassware. He had those gorgeous wine glasses that were more like fish bowls—the kind you had to nearly put your whole face in to have a sip. I couldn't help but notice that the guy had poured quite a lot in that large glass, and I had to remind myself to go easy, given that I still needed to eat. I scanned the kitchen for more food.

"Jaime's place is fantastic, don't you think?" It was the polo man again, and I got the vague sense that he was trying too hard. I followed his eyes to the enormous beams that criss-crossed throughout Jaime's kitchen and into the great room where the stone fireplace stood. He turned to look at me. "The name's Rob." He set his glass on the kitchen island—he was drinking red, too—and held out his hand. "I met Jaime through a friend of mine who helped him build this place."

His hand was large and pulpy. As I reached out to shake it, I realized that it was somewhat sweaty, too. I wanted to recoil, but didn't. *Be polite, Ann.* "I'm Ann. It's nice to meet you."

He was still holding my hand, and I was getting more uncomfortable by the minute. In contrast to my introduction to Jaime, I didn't like this lingering touch.

"So, how do you know him?" Rob asked. He had a devious look in his eyes as he casually asked the question.

"Oh… I live next door. I, uh… I own the cottage… out to the right of his." I pointed, and as I did I became somewhat embarrassed because Heart House was so small compared to Jaime's enormous castle. To distract us both I quickly grabbed a shrimp skewer when one of the dishes went sailing past me. "I really don't know him all that well, actually. I just moved here last fall, and he's been away for quite some time for his job—"

"The guy's remarkable, I know," Rob interrupted. He had a loud voice and I noticed he'd gone back to inspecting the hewn timbers above our heads.

I was suddenly very interested in what this guy had to say about Jaime. I had to dig deeper. 'Remarkable' was an understatement in my opinion, but I needed to hear what Rob knew. "What do you mean?"

Rob was shaking his head. "I don't know how he does it. I mean, he's had such a tragic past, and he somehow still manages to stay in Zen all the time. Unbelievable guy, really."

Zen?

Rob looked at me then and smiled. I suddenly had the sense that I could get any information out of Rob that I wanted. I just had to play my cards right. "Hey, do you want to head out back?" I asked. "The water is fantastic. The sounds… the waves… And Jaime has a really great deck." Speaking of whom, I still had no idea where he was, and I desperately wanted to find him.

"Sure… After you." Rob topped up his wine glass and mine, and then tightly corked a nearly full bottle of red and slipped it under his arm. He carried both glasses as I led the way to the back deck, trying to grab as much food as I could without looking like I hadn't eaten in a week.

We got to the back deck and it looked spectacular. Jaime had set up chairs and wicker lounges next to special lamps and candles, and the entire setting was akin to a posh resort in Los Cabos. Even the sandy footpath that led to the water was lined with small candles in little glass lanterns. I wondered if he had someone help him with all of his fabulous decorating. I had never encountered a man who could be so artistic and creative in his own home. Funny enough, I began to notice a few more gay men. *Is someone in his family or circle of friends gay?* I wondered. *Maybe they're the source of his fabulous decorating…*

Rob and I walked halfway down the sandy path and then stopped. Just as I leaned against a huge oak to steady my balance from what was turning out to be too much wine, I finally saw him. *Jaime.* He was down by the beach sitting around a small fire in a folding chair with about ten or twelve other people. I quickly zeroed in on a number of women who were very attractive— and very scantily clad. One of them looked to be Amanda, the girl I had met at the bonfire. She was wearing a bikini top and shorts and seemed to be the centre of attention, rocking her hips to the music and trying to keep upright in the deep, uneven sand.

And to think I was worried about wearing my sleeveless tank, I mused. I saw Amanda sit on Jaime's lap and I stiffened. Unlike the night at the bonfire, he seemed to be enjoying this attention—and he certainly made no move to get this woman off his lap. The two of them were laughing uncontrollably at something, and I wondered if she was a girlfriend now—or maybe she'd always been a friend with benefits? I relaxed slightly when I saw her turn similar attention to a few other men in the group. Shortly after, she became very affectionate with another female.

"I mean, do *you* think that's fair?"

I blinked and refocused, realizing that Rob had been talking to me and I was not listening whatsoever. "Well… um… I would say… that we need some more wine, don't you think?" I said, trying to cover my inattention. I regretted the words as soon as they were out of my mouth. I certainly did *not* need any more wine. However, it might have been just the thing to tame my uncontrollable envy. I looked down towards the beach again and noticed that Amanda was sitting on Jaime once more.

Rob grinned widely as he uncorked the bottle he had brought out with us. I tried to smile back, then closed my eyes for a moment to let the jealousy seep in. *What's wrong with me? I don't own him, and he owes me nothing—he's a free spirit, and I'm just being stupid*, I silently chided myself. *Stupid for liking him, stupid for thinking that I'm in love with him, stupid for believing it could ever work. Whatever happened to trying to forget about him?* I shook my head. Jaime obviously enjoyed being around all kinds of women, and he probably made them all feel just as special and unique as he made me feel. God, I was a fool. I closed my eyes and rubbed my eyes with my right hand.

"Here you go." Rob's voice was close, and before I could look up there was another glass of red in my hand.

I smiled up at him. *Forget Jaime*, I told myself. *It'll never happen, and there are plenty of nice men out there*. I forced my eyes to focus on Rob's face. Yes, he was nice—a true gentleman. What was I thinking, wasting my time on Jaime? I needed to direct my attention to Rob and stop staring at bikini top. *Shit, every other girl here is letting loose. Plus, a bird in the hand is worth two in the bush*, I reminded myself. It was one of my mother's favourite wisdoms, although I wasn't sure she'd approve of it being used for such justifications.

I leaned against the tree for support and tried to focus my attention on Rob. "So, tell me about yourself," I said, turning so that my back was facing the beach and the whole bonfire scene. I reached forward to touch Rob's arm in a light and casual way.

Rob started to tell me about his job at the boat dealership and about all of the interesting people he met in the business, but I was losing concentration. I was also wavering a little on my feet. I reached out to steady myself with his arm a few times, and I could tell that he was interpreting this gesture for growing interest on my part. And why not? I tried to convince myself that he was looking better and better as the night progressed.

I continued to hear girls squealing by the beach, and one particular scream pierced through the night, making everyone on the back deck look, including us. One of the girls had decided to strip right down to her bra and thong, and it appeared that she had been thrown into the water. I laughed to indicate that I thought the whole thing was funny, but I could feel a very bitter taste creeping up the back of my throat.

It was right about this time that Jaime turned towards the house and looked directly at me. I couldn't be sure if this was the first time he had actually seen me, but the alcohol gave me the necessary courage to hold his gaze. I decided to turn it into a game—who would look away first? Then I felt Rob touch my arm, and I decided to go with it. I broke the connection with Jaime to turn and face Rob. In doing so, I lost my balance and fell into him.

It actually felt good to fall into Rob's arms, and I began to wonder how the night would end. I also began to feel somewhat vindictive towards Jaime. Why that was, I couldn't be sure, but it was a release and I needed it. *Let him have his gaggle of young, slutty girls, I decided jealously. I can have my own fun, too, with or without Mr. Batten.*

"I'm so sorry, Rob. Really." I knew I was speaking louder than usual, and my brain was coherent enough to warn me that my words were coming out slowly. God, I needed water.

He smiled devilishly. "Do you want to find somewhere to sit down? Somewhere with fewer people around?" He said this with utter sweetness and I found myself liking it. "There's a little den upstairs that should be pretty private…"

I was just about to acquiesce when a voice suddenly broke in between us. "Hey, Ann—there you are!" Jaime had jogged up the path to where Rob and I were standing. He was slightly out of breath as he took a firm grip of my left arm. "And Rob… So nice to see you again." Something about Jaime's expression didn't match his words. He didn't let go of my arm, his hand firmly cupping my elbow.

I almost laughed at the irony. After months of waiting, the minute I decided I didn't want to be around Jaime, there he was. *Go, Jaime. I'm enjoying Rob now.*

Rob looked down at Jaime's hand where it held onto my arm. "Nice to see you too, Jaime. Trust life is treating you well?"

"Good so far." Jaime grinned at Rob, and then looked at me. He still hadn't let go of my arm. "Are you having a good time, Ann?"

I could sense that Rob was feeling uncomfortable with Jaime's acute presence and his firm grip on my arm. Apparently, he had no intention of letting go. Rob shifted his weight. He seemed to take the cue that Jaime wanted a minute alone. "I'm going to get us some more wine, Ann, and check on things in the den. I'll be right back." He began walking up the path towards the back deck.

Jaime, still holding onto my arm, gently pulled me towards the forest so that we were away from the path and out of other people's sight. He moved very close to me until our bodies were touching in places other than our arms.

"What are you doing?" I stammered.

"Ann, don't take this the wrong way, but I think Rob's already fed you too much to drink." He was standing so close to me that I felt I was suffocating in his aura. He smelled so good. I could feel his breath on my skin. "Rob's a nice guy, but he can be a real jerk, too. I know you don't know what I mean, but I know him and I know people who know him. Do you catch my drift? You might want to take it… slow, okay?" He chose his words carefully.

"You think I… can't take care of… of myself?" My words came out a little more sluggishly than I would have liked. "I'm a big girl, Jaime." I trumped my statement with a big grin, but then stumbled on the uneven ground. One of the straps on my blouse fell off my shoulder.

Jaime looked like he was enjoying this. He gave me one of his dazzling smiles that made my knees go weak. "I know you can take care of yourself, Ann. It's just that you look so pretty tonight. Lots of guys are going to hit on you, and not all of them will be nice guys."

And what the hell is wrong with that? I wondered. *It's not like you've paid me any attention at all tonight—not until now, just as I was starting to have fun without you. Typical man.*

He moved a little closer and stared at me so intently that it felt like a penetrating force. He glanced at my shoulder and, with a tender touch, he wrapped his fingers around the strap and delicately slid it back into place. "Your hair's straight," he observed.

I nodded. "You like it?"

"I like it when it's curly," he said, letting go of my arm. Before I could feel any sting from his words, he raised his other hand to my face and brushed it lightly across my cheek before placing some loose strands behind my ear. He was so close to my face, and my heart was pounding so loudly, that I was certain he could count the beats. His hand moved from my ear to the back of my neck, and then his fingers slowly trailed down my bare arm before he dropped his hand to my hand. My entire body was quivering. Everything seemed to be happening in such slow motion. "Be careful, and don't do anything too crazy, okay? I'll be watching."

Suddenly he let go of me and turned to walk away, leaving me feeling cold all over. *What the hell? I wondered.* As I watched Jaime's back retreat, I was burning with so much desire that I couldn't even speak. *Oh God, come back,* I urged him silently. I closed my eyes and tried to comprehend what had just happened. He was such a tease, and it was destroying me. Just when I had been ready to move on, he found a way to pull me back into his web. I wondered if he obtained some perverse pleasure in doing these things. Was he letting me know that he had more serious intentions? Or was he just being an asshole?

At that moment, Rob returned and handed me another glass of wine. Now that Jaime had broken the spell that had existed between Rob and I, I could see Rob for what he was—a sleaze ball boat salesman who was looking to get lucky. And it was not going to happen. *Not on my terms, buddy.* I asked him to hold my glass and excused myself to the ladies room. But instead of searching out a bathroom, I beelined it for the front door of the house and rushed down the driveway as quickly as I could. I just needed to be home—back at Heart House, where I could think things through. And where I could sleep this whole confusing night off.

As I stumbled over the uneven ground of my driveway, I fumbled for my keys in my pockets and began trying in vain to unlock the front door to Heart House. I dropped my keys in the mud, and as I bent to pick them up, I began feeling disoriented and woozy. I was dizzy and spinning out of control. I needed to make it to my bed, and fast. So much for tonight being a night of answers.

CHAPTER 17

Saturday morning came with a significant degree of
pain and suffering. The rain returned to accompany my
sick state of mind, and I swore up and down to myself
that I would never drink alcohol again. I hid in Heart
House for two days to avoid any possible encounter
with Jaime, and it was glaringly obvious to me that he
didn't stop by my cottage to see me, either. I packed up
and drove home to the city under dark skies on Sunday
evening. After my embarrassing stint at Jaime's place, I
couldn't help but feel like I was throwing away my
sanity—and my dignity—for a man who was more than
likely just toying with me. As I crossed the miles of
farmland and headed towards the dim glow of light
hovering over Toronto, I made the conscious decision
to stay away from the cottage in the near future and try
to focus on the humdrum of the job.

And yet, even this decision could not curtail my
incessant obsession with Jaime Batten. I simply
couldn't figure him out for the life of me. So, because I
was sure that Dr. Harris would scold me for self-
inflicted delusion if I told her, I sought out the practical
advice of my hairdresser, Suzie. I had been with her for
fifteen years, and she could be trusted like no other. She
had a matter-of-fact style, and was essentially right

most of the time. I knew she could set me straight on this one.

Over the course of her placing slips of foil in my hair, adding toner, and shampooing out the residue, I delivered my entire monologue in precise sequence. "So?" I sheepishly asked. "What's your take on all this?" I sought her eyes in the mirror, anxious for the verdict.

Suzie had a strong Spanish accent and a look that combined Cleopatra and Twiggy. "Well, he's attracted to you. The mere fact that he commented on your appearance more than once makes that obvious. And the way he needs to touch you… I don't think you should even question that."

"So what's the problem, then? He's just shy?" I was as frustrated as ever. "Playing hard to get?" *Please help me, Suzie*, my eyes pleaded with her through the mirror.

"No." She became more pensive than I had ever seen in all the years I had known her. She wrapped my head tightly in a towel and dabbed away the excess water that had started to drip down my forehead and back. I could tell she was choosing her words carefully. "It's like there's a… a *block* of some sort, or else he would have made a move on you by now, I'm sure of it. Something isn't right. I don't know what it is, Ann. Maybe he has strong feelings from a past relationship and he's still in pain. Maybe it ties in with the loss of his family; I don't know. Maybe there's something else going on in his life, and you're causing a distraction for him. All I know is that something is strange. I'm sorry I can't solve your mystery."

I groaned. "What should I do, then?"

Suzie knit her eyebrows together. "Maybe you just need to stay low on the radar for a while, and if opportunity knocks, go for it. Maybe he needs more time."

I nodded. Suzie's advice confirmed my earlier decision to stay away from Heart House for a while.

"Let's cut your hair now, honey." As she placed her delicate hands on my shoulders, I could sense some pity in her voice. I sank back in her black leather chair and as she proceeded to trim my hair. Her words tumbled around and around in my head. *Something isn't right…*

And then it came to me, clear as day. She was absolutely brilliant. Something was wrong—and that something was *me*. What I'd thought was obvious was actually the not-so-obvious source of my confusion. *He makes me think that he's attracted to me, and yet I can't really be sure of it*, I mused. *In fact, he pulls away when I think there may be more, and all I can do is wonder if it's all in my imagination. He makes me think I'm pretty, but that might be an illusion, too. What if I've grossly over-exaggerated every move he's ever made, simply because I'm attracted to him—and perhaps needy?*

As these thoughts coursed through my mind, I had a hard time looking at myself in the mirror as Suzie snipped away at my hair in comfortable silence. *I'm wanting things that don't even exist. The whole thing is a mirage, and I'm the thirsty nomad. The thirsty, stupid nomad.* I sank lower into Suzie's chair and surmised that I had been one great fool.

"Suzie, I need a change. Take four inches off. No, wait—take six."

Suzie's hands froze in mid-air as she looked at me in the mirror. She probably thought I was going insane. In fifteen years, I had never once asked for more than a trim.

I could see her lips forming the question, but I cut her off. "Just do it."

CHAPTER 18

When the Canada Day holiday arrived on the first day of July, it conveniently managed to lodge itself at the beginning of a three-day weekend. I desperately wanted to get out of the city, and I was craving Lake Huron's white caps, but I was hesitant for fear that my slightly hardened feelings would only get shattered mercilessly if I saw Jaime again. I prided myself on coping so well over the last six weeks, and on refraining from any getaway in Kincardine Township since the terrible weekend of Jaime's party. But it had been difficult to stay away. I imagined my day lilies in full bloom and thought about how spectacular their bright orange hues must look against the light blue siding of my cottage. But I needed to stop being a fool, and the only way I could do that was to park some distance between Jaime and I and get over my incessant obsession—once and for all.

The work week ended when Thursday evening arrived, and I had arranged to have a drink with Renee at one of our favourite downtown pubs. The Over Draught was Irish in origin, and we were surrounded by dark wood, big screen televisions, and cold beer on tap. With my elbow resting on the table, I was tapping my fingers against my mouth because I couldn't stop thinking about whether I should head up north for the weekend or not.

"Why don't you make a small move on him and see what happens?" Renee was direct and forward as usual.

Of course that would be her approach, I thought. She always seemed to care less about the consequences than anyone else. "No way, Renee." It was my classic retort. "I don't think I can do it. And besides, I'm trying to *forget* about this guy, remember? My feelings obviously aren't mutual, and I need to keep some distance."

"Whatever you say, Ann. But if your mind's so made up, why don't you just forget about it?" She leaned back in her chair and raised her eyebrow at me. She had me in a corner and she knew it.

But before I had to think up a plausible reply, she became distracted by some rowdy men who were drinking Stella beer at the bar. God, she had a short attention span sometimes.

In a moment she turned her attention back to me. "Listen, you don't know for sure what his feelings for you are, right? He may be playing the game. You know, playing hard to get to keep you interested for the long run. Wait it out."

"But it could take months of agony before he tries anything," I countered. "And that's *if* he tries anything—the key word here being *if*. And I'm through with putting my life on hold for men. I've been doing that way too much lately."

I could tell from her look that she wasn't convinced. Heck, I wasn't even sure that *I* was convinced.

"Then get him drunk. Now there's an idea…" she said, and I could tell that she wasn't joking. "If it's going to happen, that's when it will happen." She sat back in her chair and adjusted her blouse as she eyed some men in business suits sitting two tables over. She was expertly revealing just enough cleavage to make a man look twice without seeming sleazy about it.

I tried to imagine myself doing something similar, but the picture just couldn't form in my mind. I was cold in this regard, I knew. But I didn't have to be, did I? *Should I try to get Jaime drunk?* I wondered, mulling over Renee's suggestion. *And would that even be how I wanted to spend a potential first night with him?*

Renee rolled her eyes. "I'm not talking rip-roaring drunk, Ann." As always, she seemed to be reading my mind. I could only deduce that my face revealed everything. "I'm just talking about some wine to unravel the senses. Let the inhibitions ride. Do you know what I mean?" She was waving her hands like a gypsy putting someone in a trance. Interestingly, that's just when one of the suits finally took notice of her.

"Of course I know what you mean, Renee." I tried to look at her indignantly. "But I'm pretty sure that might just be inviting disaster."

"Well, at least you're thinking about it. You need to give it a try and see where it goes. It's just a harmless bottle of wine… and if it goes nowhere, at least you'll have your answers. *Fait accompli.* Then you can move on, maybe even sell that goddamned place. Honestly, I'm almost sorry I led you to it in the first place, because ever since you bought it, you've gotten worse. The idea was that it would make things *better* for you—and the exact opposite has occurred."

I sighed because she was right. Things had gotten out of control. My emotions were a roller coaster, and I needed to park them one way or another.

"Honey," she began again, reaching across the table and taking my hand in a way that rendered pity and softness together, "there are so many more fish in the sea. Why are you so fixated on this guy?"

Good question. I groaned and felt a concurrent pain frame my words from deep within me. "I don't know." I almost started crying. I looked up at Renee and felt a terrible hollow in my heart. "It came out of nowhere. It was instantaneous—almost like cupid came down and shot an arrow through me the very first day I saw him. It all sounds so ridiculous, I know, but it really happened like that. I mean, it was so strong and forceful. How can anyone explain that?"

Renee looked over at the man two tables over and flashed him a tremendous smile—the same smile I'd seen her use to bring men to their knees a hundred times. "I guess it was love at first sight," she said simply.

And as she said the words, something seemed to click in my heart.

***

That night I sat at my computer researching anything that had to do with the concept of love. After perusing the Internet for almost three hours, I stared at my computer screen and focused on two words.

Soul mates.

The verdict was pretty clear. Whether it was a love relationship or a platonic relationship, the research reported that certain connections could often feel deeper than others—like they had been established in the two people's souls forever. There was a reported feeling of knowing the other person for an entire lifetime—including past lives. The feeling was said to be eerie and cool, yet accompanied by a comfort brought on by knowing that the connection had been there forever. "It's like a bond that has transcended time and space," I read out loud. "There is never an end to it because your lives—present, past, and future—will always connect you to the other person in more ways than you can possibly imagine."

I had to get up from the computer. *Are Jaime and I soul mates?*

I returned a few minutes later with a mug of tea and kept reading. One theory of soul mates, as voiced by Aristophanes in Plato's Symposium, cited that humans originally consisted of four arms, four legs, and a single head made of two faces. But, fearing their power, Zeus split them all in half, condemning them to spend their lives searching for their other halves. Some people believed that souls were literally made to be the mates of other souls, in order to play certain important roles in each other's lives. I read over countless other interpretations of soul mates, and in each case, the souls seek to find their other halves in order to feel completed. When all karmic debt is purged, the two halves will fuse back together and return to their ultimate condition: being together for eternity.

Karmic debt? I'd have to ask my sister Thea about that. Was I living out some sort of punishment for a crime I had committed in a past life? Were Jaime and I destined to meet for a purpose? Were we playing out some condition set forth in our present reality in order to be fused back together in this lifetime? Or would we have to wait for another lifetime to be joined? I glanced at the clock; it read 3:17 a.m. *Time for bed,* I told myself. I needed to sleep. I had a long drive ahead of me tomorrow.

After all, I had decided to go to Heart House.

CHAPTER 19

The July heat was sweltering, and the broken air conditioner in my car left me no choice but to leave the windows down in the smog-infested traffic. A two-car pileup in the ditch left hundreds of motorists crawling along the highway, all with an array of hot tempers. I surmised that we were all equally pining for our long-awaited retreats, and the intensity of the heat combined with our collective impatience only stoked the fires of road rage.

My odometer had been sitting at zero for nearly an hour, and just when I thought I couldn't take it anymore, the distance between the stagnant cars seemed to stretch a little, showing mercy to all of us as we were allowed to begin to creep along. When I felt a breeze coming through the window, I knew we had been saved; we were finally moving and it was the most wonderful feeling in the world.

Five long hours later, I arrived at Heart House. My trunk was open in no time, and as I unpacked my supplies and clothes for the weekend, I stole a quick glance to my left. Jaime was nowhere to be seen, but the mere presence of his sporty BMW alongside his shiny pick-up truck spoke volumes. *He's home!* I felt a flutter of excitement, but turned away and forced myself to concentrate on my lilies.

***

It wasn't until the next morning, when I decided to venture down to the beach to combine catching rays and writing, that I saw him. He was out on the water sailing in his catamaran with the deftness of a professional. I smiled inwardly as I recalled how a very similar image, as seen through my kitchen window less than a year ago, had changed my life forever. He saw me on the beach and waved from a distance.

I waved back. *Don't get too excited, Ann*, I cautioned. *Focus. He's just your neighbour. Nothing more.* I looked up and noticed how the skies were crystal clear and showcasing the sun in all of its splendid glory. I set my papers down and, after organizing my towel to afford myself some comfort on the hot sand, I removed my cover-up and lay back to absorb the rays.

I let out a big sigh. *We are just going to ignore the neighbour, Ann. Keep it simple.*

It was not a day for strong breezes, although it was easy to hear the soothing waves as usual. The warmth of the sun, combined with the synchronous laps of water, began to soothe me like a lullaby, numbing my senses and luring me into a wonderfully drowsy state. I began to float far, far away. I thought I could hear someone calling me, but it was like I was attached to a hot air balloon and being carried off on the wind.

I was flying over the lake now, and I was free. Even the birds couldn't keep up with me, and I started to laugh because they were so slow. The clouds tried to capture me with in their soft embrace, but I was too strong; I told them I didn't love them and that they needed to go away. They began to cry, and rain started to pour down and soak all of the people below. But I kept laughing, because I just didn't care. All I wanted to do was keep flying and leave everyone behind. The people began to call for me, but I resisted. Suddenly I looked up and there was a black cloud looming in front of me. It scared me and I tried to turn back, but I couldn't fly anymore. I started to fall, and my arms began flailing and it became difficult to breathe. My lungs filled up with a toxic substance and it was suffocating me…

I awoke with a start, gasping.

Jaime was standing right beside me, and I screamed. "Jesus, Ann," he said, looking nearly as startled as I felt. "I was calling and calling for you."

"What the hell, Jaime? Why do you always sneak up on me like that?" My heart was racing from the adrenaline of being scared shitless by my nightmare in the sun.

I lay back down, pulled my cover-up over my body in a self-conscious way, and covered my face with my hands. When I eventually opened my eyes, I could see that he had parked his body neatly on the sand beside me. He was wearing nothing but a pair of swim shorts. He was lying on his side, twirling a piece of grass between his fingertips and looking utterly relaxed with his ankles crossed in the sand. Drops of water were glistening on his skin. It was an image out of a Nautica ad—an image that was both too casual and too poised.

"I must have fallen asleep and had a nightmare," I explained weakly. It was all I could think to say, because I really didn't know what the hell had just happened.

He laughed and smiled. "What on earth were you dreaming about?"

"Oh, I don't know. I think I was flying, and then all of a sudden I was falling." I rubbed my eyes and pushed my hair away from my face as I sat upright. "Probably just too much stress from work. I'm okay now."

I wanted to reach out and touch him because it would feel so nice, but instead I smiled and turned to gaze out at the water. Looking at him was always difficult. There always seemed to be this palpable degree of discomfort between us that was completely unexplainable. *Unless it's that eerie feeling suggested by the soul mate research*, I thought dryly. In any event, it was safer to watch the water.

I leaned back and propped myself on my elbows, keeping my focus on the horizon. The breeze began to pick up, which provided a much-needed distraction. We both stayed quiet for some time before he turned his attention back to me, sprinkling some sand on my left hand. I continued to stare at the water, attempting to ignore this intrusion despite every nerve within me alighting on fire. He seemed to enjoy this little game, as he continued to create little rivulets of sand all over my arm.

He suddenly reached up and gently turned my face towards him. "You cut your hair off."

It wasn't an accusation, but I felt like I needed to explain myself all the same. "Yeah, I did. I needed… I just needed a change, I guess." Being so close to him made my heart race.

"Let's go in the water. It'll be a riot with those waves, don't you think?"

A mixture of excitement and fear came over me. "Well," I began, my voice cracking slightly as I looked at the waves beginning to crash on shore. "I don't know. I've never been a very strong swimmer."

I was hoping to have some further discussion about this, but he quickly pulled me upright and dragged me towards the water. "Don't worry—I'll protect you," he said over the sound of the waves. "I've been swimming in these waters for far too long."

I didn't want to tell him that I hadn't yet ventured into the lake, even after having owned Heart House for nearly a year. And I wasn't sure I wanted to change that now. The cool water splashing around my ankles felt good, but I couldn't help but hesitate and yearn to go back to the shore. If it weren't for Jaime's tight grip on my wrist, I don't think I would have gone any further, infatuation or not. Yet, once the water was lapping at my thighs, I realized that it wasn't at all that scary.

The waves were warm but forceful, and were crashing rhythmically against us. At first I was pleased by the gentle force that each wave brought, but within seconds I was hit by a blast that threw me backwards and pulled me under the surface. I was terrified as I attempted to get myself oriented and upright, but I felt helpless against the churning water. Within moments, however, I felt a pair of strong arms wrap around me and pull me to the surface. I gasped for air and struggled to open my eyes.

"Ann!" Jaime cried, but there was no urgency in his voice. He was laughing naturally. "Ann—are you alright?" He was holding me against him and our wet bodies were slippery and unsteady.

Before I could answer, another surge hit us and we both went tumbling forward. I could feel the bottom of my bikini fall off, and I frantically scrambled underwater to get it back into place. It was at this point that I began to see the humour in the situation. I couldn't see, my bathing suit was falling off, and just as I was almost at the point of getting myself together again, another breaker would hit me and it would start all over again.

Eventually I got the hang of it and was able to not only anticipate, but also easily respond to, the push and pull of the waves. As I grew more accustomed to the water and learned how to handle it, I realized that I didn't want it to end. Jaime was a natural in the water, and it was absolutely marvellous to watch his hard, strong body dive towards a wave and surface moments later. I also enjoyed his sturdy arms steadying me, and on one occasion, our bodies were literally rubbing against one another. It was completely erotic and I wondered how his body was registering the moment. When we were both tired from the thrills of the waves, our wet and weary bodies made their way towards the shore.

Jaime was a few feet ahead of me, and as I looked at him I couldn't help but admire the entire package. He was running his hands through his hair when he turned around to face me. He continued to walk backwards in the water towards the shore. I wasn't sure if I was imagining it, but he seemed to be holding his gaze on my body. *God help me. What is really going on here?*

"Hey, Ann," he began, his eyes moving up to meet mine. "I was thinking of heading into town for dinner tonight. Would you like to join me?"

Is he asking me out on a date? I couldn't figure out if he had any idea how he was affecting me. Probably not. Most likely the invitation was purely platonic. I tried to think of him like a friend. Like a

Renee. Jane and Dick playing in the water, that's all. *He's just asking you to join him for dinner, Ann. There are no strings attached here*, I reminded myself.

We reached the beach and my towel felt incredibly warm and soft on my skin. The wind was steady now, and once out of the water, the cooler air immediately brought out goose bumps on my body. I waited before I spoke again, not even turning to look at him. "That would be nice, actually. Where were you thinking of going?"

As I spoke I looked up. In the sky, the seagulls had begun to circle and squawk louder than usual. Strangely enough, I couldn't help but feel like it was a subtle message. *Excitement… or a warning?*

Jaime spoke up and I turned my attention back to him. "Well, there's a nice restaurant on the water with an outdoor patio. Or we could be spontaneous and figure it out when we get there…" He gave me one of those infectious smiles as he reached over and wiped a drip of water from the bridge of my nose.

We lingered on the sand for a little while longer while the warm sun dried us. We talked about everything, from my garden and Mr. Barns to his parents and sister. He even told me about his work and some of the more scary situations he had been in. Although the mere thought of him being so close to gunfire rattled me, I listened intently. I told him about my divorce and the lawsuit, my crazy job, and my friends. In the end, it turned out to be a relaxing and pleasurable afternoon, and for once I finally felt at ease around him. The eye contact became easier, and as we exchanged stories about ourselves, we realized that we had more in common than I could ever have expected.

It was difficult to end what felt like a perfect afternoon, but errands couldn't be put off any longer. Jaime had to pick something up from the hardware store, and I desperately needed to shower and freshen up—and, most importantly, find something to wear for the evening.

As we left the beach and walked along the sandy path leading up to our cottages, he reached over and playfully put his arm around my waist. "How about you come by around seven?"

I nodded.

Then, unexpectedly, he put one arm around my shoulder and pulled me closer to him. "And next time, let's go a bit deeper."

CHAPTER 20

Elation was not a strong enough word to describe how I was feeling as I made my way back to my cottage. I brushed the sand from my toes before heading inside, then began to fret about what I was going to wear. After rifling through my drawers, I realized that my clothing dilemma was beyond description. I had packed absolutely nothing that was suitable to wear to any place fancier than Fran and Bob's store. I glanced up as a car passed by on Lake Road, and my thoughts immediately turned to Kincardine.

Twenty minutes later I was putting coins in a parking metre and praying for a miracle. I turned away from the car, squinted at the sun, and took a deep breath. Violet's Vine sat up on a hill and was surrounded by an enormous display of wind chimes. I had walked by the store on numerous occasions, and although I had been intrigued by the window displays, I had never ventured in. *Oh well, there's a first time for everything.* As I climbed a few limestone steps towards the front door, a black kitten peered out at me and beckoned me to enter. There was a pretty hand-drawn vine on the heavy wooden door, which I had to push quite firmly to open. I paused and took another deep breath. Given the aged appearance of the door and its frame, I was taking a chance shopping here at all. But my choices were pretty limited at that point; it was either Violet's Vine or I was wearing a pair of yoga pants tonight.

I entered the small store with bells jingling, and the smell of incense hit me as I passed through the heavy wooden doorway. The wood floors were ancient and creaked beneath my steps, and I could hear trickling water from little meditation fountains that were strategically placed out of sight. There was an aura of calmness to the space, and yet there was a peculiarity to it as well.

I didn't see any store attendants at first, but eventually I heard noises coming from the back, and within a few seconds a woman emerged. She walked slowly towards me in a flowing white skirt. She looked to be in her late fifties or early sixties, although it was hard to tell. Her long gray hair was tied loosely at the back of her neck, and free strands framed her oval face. I could tell that she had been remarkably beautiful once. This must be Violet.

"Hello," she said, her voice as calming as her appearance. "How can I help you?" She moved effortlessly across the room like a swan gliding across a still pond. As she neared me, her hazel eyes looked directly into mine, which immediately made me nervous. *Why does everyone do that up here?* I wondered, annoyed.

"I'm looking for something to wear for dinner. I didn't bring anything up." I cleared my throat. "What I mean is that I'm up from the city and I didn't expect to be going out for dinner, but now my neighbour has asked me to go to dinner with him and I'm stuck without anything to wear."

She was incredibly still and scrutinized me closely. I was beginning to wish I'd never come in here. "Where are you going?" She smiled as she asked the question, but it didn't help to make me feel any better.

"Well, actually, I don't really know. I'm not too familiar with Kincardine. My cottage is outside of town, on Lake Road. But I think Jaime said it was a restaurant in town on the water. I believe it has an outdoor patio." *Stop rambling, Ann. She's not going to bite you.*

"Mmmm. That would be Blakely's. That's an excellent choice by the man in question. Jaime, is it? Let me see what I can find." She began rummaging around in a few hanging racks, rhythmically glancing at items and then sliding them along the rack, one by one. After a few minutes, she looked up. "Oh, here. I think I've found the perfect thing. I just got this in the other day." She carefully pulled out a little black dress.

I stared at it with absolute delight, for although it was relatively plain, it was a unique piece because of the cut and fabric. *How did something like this end up in the middle of nowhere in a place called Violet's Vine?* I wondered, marvelling at this small town for not the first time. I hurriedly tried it on and immediately noticed how beautifully it contrasted with my sun-kissed skin and wavy blonde hair. The straps were tailored to perfection, and my breasts looked wonderful. Wow. The woman had style.

I stepped out from behind the changing curtain and looked in her direction. She was bent over, fiddling with some boxes to her right. Eventually, she stood up and faced me. She gave an almost imperceptible nod of approval.

"Do you have shoes?" She asked, standing up quickly. She was a little out of breath from being bent over. *She certainly isn't the overly friendly type*, I observed.

I told her that I didn't, and she struck gold again, pulling out a pair of dainty low-heeled sandals. I felt like Cinderella as I slipped my feet into them.

My fairy tale mood changed abruptly as I was standing at the cash. Without warning, and in a complete abrupt face from her previously detached demeanour, she took my hands in hers and looked directly into my eyes again. "Jaime Batten is a wonderful boy, but he's meant to be a free spirit, if you know what I mean."

I froze. It seemed that everyone around here knew Jaime—or at least knew *of* him. I wanted to ask for clarification, but I was suddenly very confused. My expression must have given away my thoughts because she continued, her tone suddenly dead serious.

"There is a great mystery around that family—something dark, something that you or I could never touch. But the Great Spirit is always watching—especially here in Huron, one of many places of creation." She kept a firm hold of my hands as she spoke, and shivers began to travel up my spine. I was trying to determine if she was nuts or if she really knew something that I didn't. She squeezed my hands as if to make me take special notice of her next words. "He's beautiful, that's for certain. But he cannot be reached by love until the darkness that surrounds him is resolved. Do you understand?"

I didn't.

She squeezed my hands again and then uttered six words that paralyzed me. "You are part of the darkness."

I was dumbfounded.

"I hope you'll come back to visit me again, and tell me all about your wonderful dinner."

Without a word, I took my packages and left the store, more perplexed than I had been in a long time.

CHAPTER 21

As soon as I got back to the cottage, I showered, dressed, and put on a light touch of makeup. The next hour seemed to crawl by and I watched the clock constantly. I couldn't help but ruminate about Violet's comment. *What the hell had she been talking about? And how was I part of the darkness?* It had all been so strange. When the little hand finally came to rest close to seven, I hesitated. I stood outside on my deck and listened to the water, trying to hear if a message was being sent. *How will this night end up?* I wondered.

Thinking back on my afternoon with Jaime gave me added reassurance. I was hoping that the night would go smoothly, and yet I was undeniably restless after my time spent in town. There was no denying that something was up between Jaime and me. The chemistry had been so real that I could still almost taste it, and in a very strange way I knew that something was going to happen tonight.

I stepped down off my deck and felt the cool sand envelop my feet. I carried my sandals as I made my way towards his cottage. When I approached, I could see his silhouette on his upper deck. He was very still, staring out to the lake; in fact, he seemed to be in a trance.

I waved and smiled as I emerged from the pines. There was a small pause before he spoke. He looked almost pained, but quickly changed his expression and flashed his characteristic smile. "Wow, Ann. You look beautiful." I smiled, gratified. He had no idea how much I loved it when he complimented me. I had purposely let my hair go wild for the night because I knew that was how he liked it.

He held out his hand to me and we proceeded through his house to the front of his cottage and got into his BMW. With Jaime driving, it only took about ten minutes to get to Kincardine. I cherished those minutes like they were the last ones in my life. The car was standard, and I loved watching him shift gears while he simultaneously pressed pedals with his muscular legs. He was sitting low in his seat and looking extremely svelte, and this business of fast driving was killing me. I felt like a Bond girl.

As we pulled into town, I couldn't help but notice that the nightlife was indeed very quiet here. There were a few people strolling on the sidewalks, and the odd jogger could be seen by the water or under the street lanterns. Two hanging baskets were attached to each lamppost, and the warm glow from the lanterns illuminated a cascade of petunias, zinnias, and snapdragons.

We arrived at Blakely's and were immediately seated at a lake-view table. We settled down to a bottle of champagne, an incredible dinner of shrimp and lobster, and a beautiful orange pie in the sky. I stared intently at Jaime's lips as he took a sip of champagne. They were the most perfect set of lips I had ever laid eyes on, and I couldn't help but feel a stirring between my legs as I watched him.

"Have you ever heard of the green flash?" He set his glass down on the white linen.

"The green what?" I cocked my head to the side.

"The sunset spectacle." He turned to look at the horizon and my eyes followed his. "There are disputes as to whether or not it's a myth, but I have no doubt that it's real. It can be seen at the end of sunset, just above the disk of the setting sun. Sometimes it can appear as blue, yellow, or violet, but green is most common."

I looked at the horizon but couldn't see anything.

"The sun is already gone, Ann." He smiled at me and I nervously crossed and uncrossed my legs.

"So what is it, exactly?" I asked, trying to get my mind back on what he was saying.

"When we see a sunset, the human eye is only seeing the image that is produced from the bent light rays. It's the atmosphere that's responsible for changing the light rays, and it actually has the effect of scattering more blue light than any other colour of light. The blue is diffused across the sky, while the warm reds and yellows remain to create the colour of our sunsets."

An incredibly awkward silence followed as I stared at Jaime. I could feel that our hands were actually touching as they lay motionless on the table.

Suddenly there was a cough and I could have killed the interloper. "Dessert menu, ma'am?" the waiter asked, somewhat apologetically. He seemed to be acknowledging his rude interruption into a critical moment in my life. I wasn't able to say anything.

"Thanks, Dan." Jaime's hand moved away from mine as he reached up to take the menu. When the waiter left, he turned his attention back to me and grasped my hands. "Do I get to order dessert for you, Ms. Ralston?" He cocked his head to the side and a playful smile crossed his face.

Despite my nerves, I managed to smile back and even speak intelligibly. "Absolutely. Surprise me."

He proceeded to order a decadent slice of chocolate cake and we devoured it together under candlelight. We stayed at the restaurant for a little while longer, and when the waiter picked up the bill, Jaime innocently tapped his credit card against my hand.

"Shall we go back to Lake Road, or do you want to walk around Kincardine for a bit?"

The thought of walking with him was extremely appealing, and yet I was desperate to be alone with him. I could distinctly feel the stares from people in the restaurant ever since we'd first arrived, and it had bothered me. When I'd mentioned it to Jaime, he had brushed it off in a nonchalant way and told me that staring was characteristic of small towns. "And besides," he'd added, "you're a pretty girl, Ann. Of course they're going to stare."

So now I didn't quite feel up for venturing out with him—especially when the alternative was so appealing. "Why don't we head back, and maybe we can sit by the water or something?" I didn't know what else to say, and I immediately felt foolish for even suggesting it. Surely he'd had enough of the water today.

He smiled in a mischievous way, although I wondered if it could have been my imagination. "Let's go then."

When I got back into Jaime's car, I could feel that the champagne had taken effect on me. I knew that Jaime hadn't drunk as much because he was driving, and this configuration didn't add up to my intended plan. The idea had been for *him* to have more alcohol in his system than I did. I groaned. *What would Renee suggest now?* I wondered. This evening had to end perfectly, so I spent the entire ride home thinking about what my next move should be. As we turned onto Lake Road, I spoke up. "You've never seen Heart House since Mr. Barns died. Don't you think it's about time you came in and had a look? I think you'll be surprised."

We turned in his driveway and the car came to a stop. "That sounds great, Ann," Jaime said. "It'll be a little chilly by the water anyways. Let me just grab a bottle of wine. I have something at home I've been dying to try."

Fantastic. This is working out perfectly. "As you wish, Mr. Batten." I waved my hand in the air in a cocky manner. "Get what you need and come through the back. Dinner was wonderful, by the way. Thank you for everything." I turned to look directly at him in a wanting kind of way, doing my best to imitate Renee's steamy approach with gentlemen. Whether or not he picked up on my intensity I didn't know, but it felt good to express it regardless.

"I thought it was great, too. I'll see you in a minute."

I took a deep breath and then stepped out of the car into the fresh night. We stared at each other for longer than I intended before he headed up to the front entrance of his cottage. Looking for my front door proved to be more difficult than I had anticipated, and I was thankful that he was in his cottage while I fumbled about like a moron in the bush. I was slightly intoxicated and my nerves were on fire. *This is it*, I thought. *I have to make a move.* I desperately tried to think of the advice Renee had given me, but my mind was completely blank.

When I found my front door, I quickly went inside, scrambling to light candles and tidy the place a bit. I also needed to fix myself up. I looked into the bathroom mirror and appraised my reflection. I wasn't sure if it was the alcohol or the dim lighting, but I thought I looked pretty good. In fact, I was *sure* I looked damn pretty. I tilted my head in both directions and smiled. I needed to touch up my lips, and switched to a light gloss. I had no idea where this night was going, but I didn't want to overdo it. My hair had gone extra curly during our dinner by the water, so I sprayed and scrunched it further to add to the effortless effect. At the last minute I decided to make my eyes look just a little bit smoky. *Careful, Ann.*

I heard my back door open and I knew he was inside. My heart was pounding, but I knew I somehow needed to regain control over myself. Sounds followed him through my kitchen as he helped himself to my drawers. I heard him locate a corkscrew, and within seconds came the sound of a cork popping out of a wine bottle. "Hey, Ann, I've got the wine. Where are you?" he called out.

I emerged from the bathroom and descended the stairs to greet him. He didn't seem to take any notice of my appearance this time, and that concerned me. But we'd spent a lot of time together today, so maybe I was expecting too much. Then again, maybe I overdid it with the smoky eyes. *Damn it, Ann*, I reprimanded. *You know he likes the natural look.* I decided to ignore the nagging feeling.

We sat on the couch and he proceeded to compliment me on how great the place looked. He went on to tell me about the history of the area, and about some of the local residents whose families had been here for over a hundred years. He brought up the name of a small resort that had been in the area for decades. "Birch Tree Resort. Have you seen it yet? It's just up the road."

I watched how he bit his lower lip as he said it, and then quickly distracted himself by filling up our glasses with wine. He leaned back on my couch and appeared nervous for the first time since I had met him.

"It's been around for a long time. Like I said, there's a lot of history around here."

I told him I hadn't seen the resort, but that I was intrigued. I gave him my warmest smile to let him know that I was being genuine. Even still, Jaime continued to look uneasy, and there was a definite discomfort permeating the air. I became tense as well, and wondered if this was the moment when he'd tell me good night ole buddy ole pal. But thankfully the moment passed, and we spent the next half hour chatting about the history of Kincardine.

When it was almost eleven o'clock, he looked at his watch. He swigged the last of his wine and then spoke the dreaded words. "Am I ever bagged! I think it's time to go to bed." He got up and stretched, then started collecting our wine glasses to bring them into the kitchen.

I was overcome with confusion, but I knew that I couldn't let this opportunity get away from me. Not if it meant another undefined stretch of time spent obsessing over Jaime's feelings and banging my head against a wall. I knew I had to do something to put an end to this madness of not knowing, but what? As I walked with him toward the back door, I knew that if I let this precious moment escape, I would never forgive myself. And yet, I didn't have the courage to make a move. I was also acutely aware of the possibility that he may not have wanted something to happen as much as I did, and if that was the case, could I bear the consequences? *Damn it all, why isn't he making a move?*

The Huron breeze was refreshing, and yet it hit us with such force that when we exited the cottage it almost blew me over. The breeze's eerie howling seemed to exaggerate the strangeness between us. *Am I the only one feeling this discomfort? How could this special moment be so lacking in grace?*

We walked down my steps towards the sand, and as I listened to the whitecaps crash against the shore, I could sense that he was just as uncomfortable as I was. When we approached the path that joined our properties, he turned to me. He took my hand and spoke in the lightest of whispers. *It was a great night… wonderful… it felt so good to be with you.* Did he really say all this?

I stared into his eyes and tried to ignore the terrible need I felt to walk away, as that would just be easier. But I wanted him so badly. And then, within seconds, I finally gave way to my deepest desires and moved in on him, pressing my lips to his and pulling my body hard against him. There was a palpable moment when his body struggled against mine before he finally gave in and opened his mouth, parting his lips against mine and responding in resonance to my pace.

I pushed myself against his body and dug deep, clawing at his skin. Our mouths were moving in unison, and my body was on fire and wanting more—so much more. Every switch had been flipped inside of me, and I was aching from top to bottom. His lips remained soft, but directed, and one of his arms came around to the small of my back. He brought my hips towards him, hard, letting me truly feel him. And I wanted more. We were both breathing heavily, and although I didn't want to abandon his mouth, my lips eventually left his and found their way down his neck. He tasted so good, and I knew that it had to happen. My body was ready to consume him, poised to envelop and devour him. He needed to take me there, right then, on the ground.

And then the absolutely unthinkable happened.

His body was suddenly absent from mine, and it felt like I was stumbling off a cliff face. In my mind I was falling fast and I couldn't stop. *God, help me, please*, I begged—but I was all too aware that nobody was hearing my plea. Jaime had pulled away from me, hard and fast. *But why? Jaime, why?*

Standing several feet away from me now, his hands were raised to his face, rubbing his temples and covering his eyes. He grabbed violently at a branch and snapped it over his knee. For the first time since I'd met him, he scared me. I stood motionless where he had left me, my breathing coming in long gasps. I was hurt and absolutely speechless. What could I say? What had I done wrong? It was my worst nightmare, my black cloud come true. But somehow a part of me had already known that this was going to happen.

It took a moment, but he finally walked back towards me, reached forward, and held me gently by my shoulders. I didn't want to hear what he was going to say. "Ann, I can't. I'm… uh… I'm in a relationship. I'm sorry. I can't do this."

The words hurt, but I wasn't too upset—at least, not initially. And that was because, for some unexplainable reason, I had every confidence in the world that our love and attraction would transcend this so-called relationship. Yes, we would get through the emotional rollercoaster and come out alive. Yes, we would hurt other people, but our twin souls couldn't be denied, could they? People would understand; it was an ethereal thing.

And then he spoke again. It came out as a hoarse whisper, and I wasn't sure if I really heard him. "Ann. I'm…." There was a long moment of hesitation. I was hanging onto every word. "I'm with a… a man. I'm sorry, Ann… I'm really sorry."

There was a glimpse in my memory of the gay men at his party, and as the wind blew fiercely from the shore, I tried to guess if the velocity would have some bearing on the weather for tomorrow.

Then suddenly there was a lump at the back of my throat, and I swallowed reluctantly. That was where my recollection ended. I must have extricated myself from that scene somehow, but I could not recall what happened after that. I think there was more wine involved, and a healthy dose of self-pity, because the next thing I knew, it was five hours later and I was lying on my bed, staring up to the ceiling. My wavy hair was spread out across the pillows, and my tears had long since evaporated from my pained face.

There was to be no more sadness. It was time to say goodnight… and goodbye.

CHAPTER 22

The pounding in my head was killing me. I needed to get up and retrieve some Tylenol, but my body was limp and felt foul. Sick with disease. Impurity. *Is any sick among you? Let him call for the elders of the church; and Let them pray over him, anointing him with oil in the name of the Lord: And the prayer of faith shall save the sick, and the Lord shall raise him up; and if he has committed sins, they shall be forgiven him.* The bible verse came back to me in a rush.

Will Jaime be forgiven for the sin he committed against me? I wondered as I tried to find a cooler place on my pillow. I moved in that direction, feeling with my hands like I was sightless. The pounding wouldn't stop, and then there was banging and I was confusing the two as they cornered me. I was begging for it to stop. *Have mercy upon thyself.*

"Ann, I'm coming in." His voice, and his words, made me freeze. *No. Oh, God, I didn't lock the doors. Go away. Why is he here?*

"Ann!" he yelled again, a little louder this time, and there was a sharp ringing in my ears. It was all hurting so much. That explained the double thumping and banging. He had been at the deck doors. "I need to talk to you. Listen, please come out. I don't want to come upstairs to the bedroom. Please."

Of course not… Why would you want to come into the bedroom? For 'tis a ghastly place where a woman sleeps? Fuck off Jaime, and leave my house. I felt a pang of nausea and thought about running to the bathroom. A cold sweat formed across my temples as I scanned the room for a garbage can, but within seconds the feeling thankfully passed.

"I'm not leaving, Ann. Not until I speak with you."

I wondered if he was screwing another cop. And then I remembered the pretty boys at his party. Could it have been one of them? I remembered Siobhan's curt glances, and there seemed to be some understanding now. She knew, and she'd additionally known about me. She'd read me so well and sensed my attraction to Jaime. What could she say to me other than warn me indirectly through her acerbic features? She'd aptly conveyed the pain I would soon bear.

"Fucking Christ… Ann, I'm coming up." I had never seen this side of him before. It wasn't like him to swear. His impatience with me was obviously growing; it was crawling across the floor, up the stairs, and towards my bedroom. And then again, I had never been so eager to piss him off.

I thought about how immature I was being, hiding in my bedroom like a child on the first day of school. I don't know how I did it, given my sickened state of mind, but I finally managed to pull myself together into some haphazard configuration. I placed my scrawny body in the doorway of my bedroom, slumped against the frame, and crossed my arms in front of me as if to protect myself. I was wearing a tank, no bra, with my oversized pyjama bottoms hanging low on my hips. I looked down and saw my hems crumpled on the floor. I had not a care in the world at this point. I didn't have anything to say, so I just stared down at him as he stood at the foot of the stairs.

"Jesus, Ann. You look like hell."

No comment.

"Can we at least talk about this?" His hands were on his hips and I could see that he was having trouble making eye contact with me. Instead, he chose to avert his eyes towards the lake, looking out my back windows as he spoke. "This is extremely difficult for me. Things got out of hand last night. I don't really know how…" He was running his hand through his hair as he said this. "You're attractive in a very special way to me. I can't really explain it."

More silence.

"I'm sorry." He sighed heavily and placed his hands in his back jean pockets as he turned his face up to look at me.

I truly could not make heads or tails of what he was saying. "How can you be attracted to a female if you're gay?" I quipped. I didn't understand it one bit.

He took some time in answering. "Lots of gay men can be attracted to women. It happens to some… some of us." He looked down at the floor and shuffled his feet. I could see that he was uncomfortable with the way this conversation was heading, but I didn't care.

"Bullshit. Then you're bisexual," I said matter-of-factly.

"I'm not bisexual." He emphasized the word 'not'.

Then what the hell are you, Jaime Batten? I seethed silently. *Some mixed up jerk that toys with women's hearts and leaves them standing at the county covered bridge and never comes back? Are you the type of man who is so insecure that he needs everyone to love him and fawn over him—including vulnerable women whom he has absolutely no interest in? I* lowered my head and placed a hand over my eyes. My other arm remained crossed against my braless chest. I didn't know what else to do. After all, what was there to say to this man?

"You can't be attracted to both men and women, Jaime. And if you are, I believe the correct term for it is *bisexual.*" I enunciated the last word slowly and loudly.

He said nothing.

"How can you say you're not?" I was getting angry now and started to yell. "Why did you kiss me? Were you feeling sorry for me?" I was out of control, half crying with arms flailing.

"I admit, it startled me at first." He paused and I was afraid of what he was going to say next. "I *wanted* to kiss you. Believe me when I say that, okay? Something was different with me last night. I can't explain it."

My mind was dense and thick, and I could only recall a patchy sketch of the night before. But I clearly remembered how his body had responded when we were kissing. That was a given. *Throw him a curveball.* "Then why did you stop?"

His body either twitched or quivered at the very moment I asked the question. He turned away from me and, placing his hands on the back door, he leaned against the glass. He stared out the window for the longest time before he uttered his carefully chosen answer. "Because I *had* to stop. It just can't be."

Because he *had* to stop? *How much more of this can I take?*

He seemed to sense my confusion, because he attempted to clarify. "I told you I'm in a relationship. Did I not say that?" He was getting on the defensive now, and the combination of my anger and his arrogance was not boding well for him.

Should I push the envelope just a little further? I contemplated and decided to do it. *Leave this battlefield with no stone left unturned, Ann.* "Fine. Then are you saying that if you weren't in a relationship, the night would have turned out differently? Would you have made love to me, Jaime Batten?" My hand remained on my forehead. I felt like I was turning into Renee, and I was feeling sick all over again.

"I don't know." He looked frustrated. "Probably not." He heaved a huge sigh, and I could tell that he didn't want to talk about this anymore. He'd come over to pay his respects, say his apologies, and leave—and I was dwelling on it, asking more questions, wanting more answers. But I needed information. I was obsessed, and I wasn't going to let this go.

I was also hurting badly inside, and the pain seemed to grow stronger with each passing minute. I wanted him to stay and be near me, but I also needed him to leave. It was the worst dichotomy I'd ever experienced.

"Thanks for coming by, Jaime." I took a few shaky steps down towards where he was standing. "I think I'd like to be alone now, if you don't mind. So I'm asking you to leave. Now." I raised my voice and pointed to the back doors.

He turned from the window and looked at me, and I felt that familiar gnawing deep within. I could feel electricity between us, pulling us together, and yet we were fighting it tremendously in order to maintain a very important and much-needed distance. It was such a strange, inexplicable feeling. The most bizarre thing was that I could almost decipher, in some irrational way, that it was not one-sided, and yet I was sure I'd never know because the moment could not be put into words.

Silence and some sort of eerie knowing filled my chest. As I crawled back into bed, all I could think was that Violet had been right. Because from that moment forward, the darkness overcame me.

CHAPTER 23

The wind was fierce the next day, and it seemed to resonate with my foul mood. It was next to impossible to relax at the beach with everything flying around in a semi-hurricane state, not to mention the sand that was being whipped into my eyes with a horrific sting. My papers flew everywhere, and I wanted to cry because I had no control over anything. I was left with no choice but to leave and try to find some solace on my deck to continue writing. Just as I lowered myself into my chaise lounge, I heard a door slam. It had come from Jaime's house, and when I looked up I saw his figure walking down towards his beach. *Perhaps he'll take his boat out in this wind and drown.*

There was an unfortunate break in the trees which gave me a clear view of him—and that meant I was exposed to his view, too. I considered going into the cottage, but my ego patted my back and told me to stand my ground. The last thing I would do was compromise something that I was enjoying just because someone else was making me uncomfortable. Screw him. He could leave. In fact, I considered staring him down to the point of scaring him off. My bravery was building, and for some strange reason it excited me. Sure enough, he looked up at that moment, and I froze.

My reflexes kicked in and I immediately looked down at my papers. *Damn him for looking.*

I waited a few minutes before choosing to glance up again, and I noticed that he had manoeuvred himself into his boat and was busy fiddling with something at the stern. He stood up and rubbed his hands together to brush off some sort of filth, and then proceeded to inspect his boat with his back to me. He had no shirt on and, of course, I couldn't help but stare because he looked like a bronzed god. He started to turn towards me again, and I quickly laid my head back and closed my eyes. *Another close call. Let him think I'm sun tanning and couldn't care less about him.*

I kept my eyes shut and wandered back to our moment last night by the trees. Our kiss was still vivid in my mind, and I could recall the exact feeling of his lips parting and then taking hold of mine, of his hands moving and exploring my body, of his body responding to me, and of feeling every bump and ridge when he pulled me against him. It just didn't make sense. My God, he couldn't be *gay*. If anything, he had to be bisexual.

It was then that I started to imagine Jaime with a man. I was in a semi-slumber state, and the visions flowed easily. I pictured him in Heart House, on my couch, his beautiful hand reaching up to graze another man's cheek and play with his hair. I could see him pulling the other man towards him, and their faces coming close together as light kisses heightened the intensity that was emerging between them. The kissing was becoming more powerful, and I could see Jaime slowly open his robe and gently ease it off. They were both naked now, and the other man was moving up against Jaime, their hands wild and frantic for each other, grasping and moving to each other's delight. The other man began kissing Jaime's chest, moving slowly to his navel and then kissing and exploring his way around the inside of Jaime's muscular legs. Jaime was on fire now and writhing uncontrollably. He was aching severely, and he gently guided the man's head in the direction that he so desired.

The man sensed his need and paused, his hand carefully gliding across Jaime's stomach and eventually downwards. He effortlessly grasped Jaime's prize in a delicate way. The rhythm was steady but strong, and the man's movement was perfect—at least for Jaime, whose face was now contorting as his pleasure was escalating. Both of their bodies moved in unison. Jaime stroked the other man's hair, but could barely hold any degree of concentration. He arched his hips upwards so that the other man could take in more of him. The other man held his pace and gave Jaime what he wanted and they looked beautiful together. When it was finished, Jaime lay his head back on the pillow and closed his eyes. The other man gave a small sigh of pleasure from knowing that he could please Jaime so well.

I suddenly opened my eyes and blinked at the bright sunshine. Getting up from my lounge chair, I walked into my cottage and headed for the bathroom. I thought I was going to be sick.

CHAPTER 24

Lake Road extended for another ten miles beyond my cottage. It meandered past a haphazard arrangement of century-old cottages and twisting pines. Some of the cottages were simple—ancient clapboard structures of about five hundred square feet—while others were contemporary multi-level mansions like Jaime's.

Walking down this peaceful road became a necessity for me after the fiasco with Jaime. It had only been a couple of weeks, but I carried around a painful wound that seemed to linger and swell each day. Jaime had thankfully left on a work mission, and this allowed me some much-needed space to sort out my thoughts. Again. The Huron shores provided a degree of healing, and most importantly I needed to be alone to come to terms with my feelings, for I feared that I had lost complete sight of who I really was. Never mind seeing the forest for the trees; I couldn't even see the damn trees.

A pair of chipmunks scurried across the road and rustled under the brush, the pitter patter of their tiny feet masked by cicadas crying in the heat. It was certainly another warm Lake Huron day. The same chipmunks scampered out again, and I watched how they made their way south towards an expanse of green grass that lay up ahead. As I meandered around a kink in the road, the trees parted to reveal a quaint but sizeable cottage resort.

This must be Birch Tree Resort, I realized. I winced as I remembered how Jaime had told me about this place on that ill-fated night. Renovated with a sprinkling of modern cottages and nicely tended rows of perennials, the place looked like something out of Homes and Gardens magazine. I wandered around for a few minutes, captivated by the beauty of the place. In particular there was a gorgeous old stone well that had been kept in beautiful repair. I couldn't stop myself from leaning over it and peering deep inside. There was a surprising burst of cool air coming up from its depths. I shivered and continued wandering.

According to one of the dozen or so historical plaques and glass exhibit cases, the resort had opened its doors sometime in the 1930s to a flurry of upscale folks from Toronto, as well as those from the nearby American border towns. Eager to showcase their wealth and acquire an even greater network of friends and associates, various lineages bearing the auspicious names of Rossford and Fitzpatrick chose this destination on a yearly basis. Relaxation, freedom from care, and sheer pleasure became the resort's top selling features, along with the jitterbug, square dancing, and daily cribbage tournaments.

"This was quite the place, in its heyday."

I was startled by the voice. I turned to find a fairly old gentleman standing about eight feet behind me. With some degree of frailty, he was leaning against his wooden cane. He was wearing a long-sleeved shirt and a beige checkered vest, and I wondered if he was feeling rather warm given the weather. He was grinning a grin that stretched up to a remarkable set of twinkling blue eyes.

"Pardon my intrusion, but I couldn't help but notice you reading the information on the Birch," he explained.

I reciprocated with a gracious smile. "It's no intrusion," I assured. "I was just startled because I didn't think I'd run into anyone else here."

He took a few slow steps towards me. He had a limp and was moving with care.

"I was a busboy here in the late forties. Name's McKay. Harold McKay." His voice was hoarse and I wondered if he had smoked for many years. He held out his hand to me and we exchanged a light shake.

"It was after the war, and we were finally getting back to running things the way they had been before the war started. Both my mother and father worked here, so I grew up here as a young lad." He tilted his head and his left hand rubbed a spot above his temple, which was littered with brown spots from the sun. *No doubt he's a long-time resident of the Huron beaches*, I thought.

"This place holds special memories for me," Harold went on. "When I walk past, I can almost hear the sounds of days gone by." He was still smiling, and there was a gentle sweetness about him. "I hope you don't think I'm a crazy old man." I smiled and shook my head no. I wasn't thinking that at all, but I did register that this encounter was far from ordinary. We were standing in what was almost an awkward silence when an old newsletter encased in glass caught his attention. He stared at it intently for a time, and then cleared his throat. "Well, look at that. 'Mia Stohm wins the beauty contest. 1947'," he read. "Son of a gun."

I shuffled my feet in the gravel as he went on to tell me about a beautiful young girl named Mia Stohm. She was the daughter of George and Ida, regulars from Detroit who had frequented the Birch Tree resort every summer long ago. He told me that as a busboy, he and the other employees would wait with anticipation until Mr. Stohm's Lincoln K-Series drove through the front gates of the lodge every July. He talked about how he and the boys—other employees of Birch Tree—would peer out from behind the fence off the kitchen to admire Mia, the most beautiful girl they'd ever encountered in real life.

"She was a combination of Lana Turner and Loretta Young, and petite and quiet as could be. She had the poise and gracefulness of a ballerina, but if you looked deep into her eyes, you could see that there was a fierce intelligence there, almost like a tigress. She wasn't like the other silly debutantes, who would always be gossiping about nonsense. No, not Mia. She would only listen, making her own mental calculations. She really was an enigma."

I could see that he was tiring in the sun. We moved to a small bench to sit down. There was no doubt that he needed the shade.

He looked up towards the tops of the pines and paused, a sober shadow encasing his face. "But everything changed, of course, when Jaime arrived," the old man continued.

Did he say Jaime? My heart sped up, if only for a second, and I experienced a very strange feeling of warped time—some palpable halt in this very strange universe. I felt blood draining away from every capillary in my body at the very moment this old man mentioned the name Jaime. My hand instinctively reached up to touch my throat. I was staring straight ahead, my eyes registering nothing, but somehow I knew that he was watching me intently—watching how my nervous hand stroked my skin as if to soothe me in some cataleptic way. Why? He couldn't have known I'd react that way—could he?

Jaime? Why could he not have said a different name, like John or Brian? My mind registered the eerie coincidence at the same time I directed my head to look at the man and speak. "Who was Jaime?" My voice was barely audible. My hands moved to grip the edges of the bench.

"Well, Jaime was the young man who swept Mia off her feet, of course." Harold shifted in his seat, and I could see that he was getting uncomfortable in the heat. Sweat was now showing on his forehead, and he pulled out his handkerchief and mopped his brow. "But darned if I can remember what his surname was. Let me think, now…" He was muttering to himself and staring into the trees.

It seemed that my heart might stop beating if he couldn't remember soon.

"Jaime… uh… Lark, I think," he eventually said. "Or was it Fitzpatrick? No, no, he wasn't a Fitzpatrick. He was much too handsome for that, and he didn't have the Fitzpatrick double chin." He chuckled as he wiped his face again. "Goodness, dear, I'm truly sorry, but I think it's high time I get out of the heat and head back home for a nap. I think I need some lemonade, and maybe even a little gin. But I'd be happy to tell you all about Jaime and Mia some other day, if we ever meet again."

Yes, I thought. *Please do.* "I hope we will meet again, Mr. McKay," I stammered. I helped him to his feet and watched him disappear down a faint pathway through the woods.

The walk back to my cottage somehow didn't register in my mind. I was lost in thought when I suddenly remembered something.

Initials carved into a tree.

CHAPTER 25

For many weekends afterwards, I walked down Lake Road hoping to run into Harold again, and yet I never saw him. It may have been a coincidence, but the initials on the tree that stood between Jaime's property and mine clearly had an MS and a JB. It could have been anyone that had carved those letters, and yet I felt certain that I knew exactly what they stood for—and that there was a greater connection. MS and JB. Mia Stohm and Jaime Batten.

The next few months became an endless sea of torment for me. It was my decision to refrain from speaking with Jaime, and he was well aware of my intent to create an abrupt closure of our friendship. I sensed that he was uncomfortable with this arrangement, and I may have perceived some form of emotion or trace of hurt on his face, but I couldn't be certain. His most recent work excursion had been short, and he was back at Lake Huron not long after my encounter with Harold. We had become silent strangers, and the separation was more than painful. At times, I felt like I was on fire; I was acutely aware of every move he made, but my external façade didn't let on. From behind my curtains I saw him tinkering on his boat, casting his fishing line, skipping stones. I would hear his back door open and close, and then listen intently as his footsteps made contact with his deck. I heard his back trunk slam shut on the BMW, and I listened as the engine of his pickup truck roared to life. I left my windows open on purpose, just to feel connected to him through these sounds—even though my rational mind chastised me for being so weak.

There were days when I wondered if he thought about me, and the agony of not knowing rattled me even more. There were no more waves in greeting or farewell, but on occasion we would lock eyes and hold an intense stare across a distance of thirty feet. Those moments were the worst for me.

Time seemed to stand still and I walked in a slumber, never knowing if I was coming or going— until the day Renee came up, that is. She was business as usual, fussing about in my kitchen as I vaguely paid attention. I knew that the doors on my cupboards were opening and closing as she methodically stocked the shelves. *This is a complete waste of time, Renee*, I sulked silently. *I have absolutely no intentions of eating.* And with that thought, she stopped her bustling, turned to face me, and leaned back against my counter. I looked up at her, as if on cue, and noticed for the first time that she wasn't wearing heels.

"Look at you." She folded her arms across her chest and looked annoyed.

I didn't want to entertain this conversation, so I looked away again. My kitchen window was open and the thought occurred to me that the waves were unusually rough.

"This is absolutely sick, Ann. And *you're* sick. You need to get some help. You look like you haven't showered in a week."

She came over and sat down at the table next to me. I only became aware that I had started to cry when Renee wiped away the wetness from my cheek. At least I knew a piece of me was still alive.

"You should have gotten more help after the divorce. You're turning into a train wreck. Are you still seeing Dr. Harris?" she asked.

I shook my head no. I had stopped going to Dr. Harris when I realized that I couldn't even follow her simple instructions to write down what was in my heart.

"Well, you should start again." She took my hands in hers. "Listen… at one point or another we all think we've found the perfect love, and then it doesn't work out. It happens to us all, Ann. You just haven't had it happen to you as much as the rest of us have, and that's why it's hurting so badly now. So consider yourself lucky and forget about him."

I turned to face Renee. I'd never felt so ugly and inferior as I did at that moment. I knew I had let myself go and that I was more or less falling apart, and yet, despite my rational mind reiterating exactly what Renee had just said, I couldn't get the physical part of my body to respond in unison. I felt like a tug boat stuck in the mud, and it was frustrating to have no control when

I knew I should. There was no doubt in my mind; I was severely depressed.

"I don't know how to explain it, Renee. I just can't get him out of my head. And it's not like other disappointments; this time it feels so different. It's invasive—like a cancer sucking the life out of me."

Renee made a disgusted face. "For Christ's sake, Ann." She sighed in frustration and shook her head.

Suddenly a terrible sense of injustice was triggered inside of me. Why couldn't she be more supportive? I squeezed her hands tightly. "You think I don't want this to go away? You think I should sell this place and move to some other part of the country? What the hell, Renee? You think that will make me forget this whole thing? It won't, believe me. I'm going to be stuck with this shit forever. Something is different here; I can't explain it, but I do know the difference. Believe me when I say that."

Renee reached out and took hold of me. The tears were streaming down my face and my voice was breaking, but I couldn't stop talking.

"There's also weird crap going on. Coincidences that can't be explained. Do you know what I'm saying? Things are coming together that shouldn't be together. Bizarre things are popping up out of nowhere and freaking me out. It's like a puzzle." I wanted to tell her about Birch Tree Resort and Harold, about the initials carved into the tree and about the déjà vu and eerie familiarity of the place, but Renee interrupted me before I could go on.

"He's gay, Ann—that's the fucking difference." She was calm, but her arms held me in a firm grip, and I hated her for it. Regardless, her statement was strong and I'd needed to hear it. I needed to feel her shaking the craziness out of me.

"I need to go for a walk," I said, pulling myself away. The chair squeaked against the floorboards as I stood and walked towards my front door. After slamming it shut, I walked a few more feet to Lake Road. I decided to take the opposite direction and head north, away from Jaime's house and Birch Tree Resort. This way would eventually lead to the public beach, but at that point I could have walked to China and never come back for all I cared.

I hated Renee. I hated Jaime. I would have hated anyone who crossed my path. I hated the world. My anger was so strong I began to feel elated by it—it was almost as if some strange power from within was taking over, guiding and reminding me that I didn't have to stand for this yet again. I was coming to terms with making some strong, solid decisions, and the best thing to do right now was to walk away. Renee was right—I should leave. That was the answer.

I would leave and I would never come back.

CHAPTER 26

My emotional disaster zone continued for several more months, but in the end I decided not to sell the cottage. Not yet. Instead, I had Renee take control of it and rent it to whomever. Renee interpreted this as a continuing saga of not letting go, but in the end she agreed and followed through. It had a strong appeal to potential renters who were easily drawn by the sunsets, and the rental income that I shared with Renee was an additional bonus. I completely immersed myself in work over the winter, and took trips whenever I could. There wasn't a day that I didn't think about Jaime, but the pain eventually became bearable, and on the whole I was pleased with myself for not falling down some sinkhole to hell and requiring massive amounts of medication to keep me sane.

I stayed away from Lake Huron for almost a year, and although I dearly missed the beauty of that part of the country, I made up for it by researching travel destinations that might somehow duplicate the beauty of the Huron shores.

There were even a few brief relationships that came and went. They were short lived and sweet, and they all ended when the men tried to carry things to a level that most women would want but that I couldn't bring myself to commit to. I knew my mother would have loved each and every one of them, but my feelings were virtually numb and the last thing I wanted to do was lead some poor soul astray. There was no need to make that same mistake twice. Sometimes, I would stare across a table into their eyes and try to feel some sort of sentiment in my veins. Even though I would patiently wait to be overwhelmed by emotion, the feelings never came. I tried to picture spending lazy Sunday mornings sipping coffee in bed with each of these men. It was a pretty picture, and yet within seconds the fellow would evaporate from the vision and I would be sipping coffee alone, and feeling all the happier for it. Thus, like the ones before them, each man came and went.

And so it came to be that after an empty summer and during the next fierce and cold long winter, I was feeling the need to go someplace warm. I pictured a seaside resort with a sandy place to nestle my toes, and so I arranged lunch with Gloria. She had travelled extensively and always had great recommendations.

It was a nasty, cold Friday in the middle of a snowstorm when we chose to meet. I couldn't help but smile as I watched her enter the restaurant, stamping heaps of snow from her boots and cursing incessantly about the winter winds. She was always so serious when she spoke, and unbeknownst to her, the drama and exaggeration of her speech made her incredibly funny and enjoyable to be with. She was overweight and couldn't help but brush against people as she made her way to our table. I watched with delight as a few annoyed faces looked up when their napkins fell to the ground and their tables got jostled.

"This is ridiculous." She shook her frizzy head and flakes of snow flew everywhere. "What is with this goddamned snow? I hate this shit. I might as well move to Florida with my parents."

The corners of my mouth spontaneously turned upwards. I couldn't help but smile when I was around Gloria. "How are you otherwise?"

"Fine. And you? I see you've put on some weight—finally. You don't look like a waif anymore."

More than anything, I loved that Gloria was so level headed and honest when she spoke. "I didn't look like a waif, Gloria," I protested weakly, knowing that she was right. I looked down and mindlessly fiddled with the napkin in my lap.

"You did! You looked like you weighed about ninety pounds. What are you having?" She held up the menu in front of her so that I couldn't see her face. "Jesus, I'm starving. Do they have good food here?"

We both settled for omelettes—the specialty of the house—and white wine spritzers.

"I ran into Renee," she said as she dabbed at her wet hair with her napkin.

"Really?" I said. It had been a few weeks since I'd seen Renee last. To be honest, I was doing my best to avoid her disapproving presence. "What's up with her?"

"Not much, but she ran into your friend. You know, that fellow who lives next door to your cottage? What's his name?"

There was a moment of hesitation, and a slight tug at my nerve endings, but all in all, it wasn't the disaster it could have been. I cleared my throat. "Jaime," I said dully.

"Yep, that's the one. She says he's been taking care of your cottage. And apparently he asked about you. He wants to know if you'll be coming back. How long has it been? Two years?"

"One and a half." As I muttered these simple words, I felt it all coming back. *It doesn't mean anything, Ann. Focus.* Yet emotions were coursing through my body like I was an ignited torch. My parasympathetic nervous system was moving like wooden dominoes falling from head to toe. I tucked a strand of hair behind my ear, but it fell back into my eyes. Ever since I'd stopped going to Suzie on account of my depression, it was getting harder and harder to keep my unruly waves under control. I looked at Gloria. "I didn't ask him to look after my cottage. Did Renee put him up to that?"

"Relax," Gloria piped back. "Renee didn't ask him to do anything. He's doing it of his own accord, I guess. He even showed her pictures of your gardens from the summer. I guess he's been looking after them so they wouldn't go to ruin while you're away."

I wanted this conversation to stop, and yet I also wanted more. There was an edge to this conversation, a reality that was pulling me in different directions. It was painfully alluring and dangerous at the same time.

"He also fixed your deck. And the most bizarre thing of all…." Gloria paused momentarily, and I was hanging onto her words in a paralytic state. She fiddled with her omelette and swirled a potato wedge in a pool of ketchup. Her mouth was partially full as she continued. "That wooden heart somehow fell off your front door and went missing for the longest time. Renee thought one of the renters must have taken it, but Jaime found it somewhere and nailed it back up."

The hair on the back of my neck rose. We ate in silence for the next several minutes and I wondered if she was thinking the same thing as I was. *Why do things like this happen?* It was like the universe was playing a mean trick on me, and I was the perpetual butt of a cosmic joke. *Enough of this*, I thought. I carefully placed my fork and knife on my plate and decided to change the subject. "I'm thinking of going to Grand Cayman and I wanted to get your opinion."

Gloria's eyebrows immediately shot up. "It's a wonderful place! The beaches are beautiful." She was speaking with her mouth full again.

"I'm looking for a quiet place to relax and take it easy. I'm thinking of staying at the Westin and booking a deluxe suite."

Her eyes immediately narrowed. "Why a suite? You don't need all that room, and besides, it will cost you a fortune. You'll spend most of your time at the beach or by the pool anyways. Just book a studio."

I leaned back and stared out the window as I finished my spritzer. I didn't say anything more about it to Gloria. I had plans to hunt some prey, and any potential short-term prospects would most certainly appreciate an impressive-looking suite. I was still holding onto the hope that eventually I would find someone who'd make me forget about Jaime altogether.

"Renee said your friend Jaime would be going away for a while."

God, why did she have to bring him up again? "That's nice." I smiled ever so slightly with a hint of sarcasm. And then I stared across the room at the flat screen above the bar and turned my thoughts back to Grand Cayman.

CHAPTER 27

It turned out to be more beautiful than I had imagined. Grand Cayman was one of three islands that, together with Cayman Brac and Little Cayman, formed a paradise approximately five hundred miles south of Miami. The sun-kissed beaches and aqua blue waters attracted thousands of tourists every year, and any sports enthusiast would not be disappointed by the snorkelling and best scuba diving available. North Sound was particularly famous for its shallow reef protected lagoon, and it was here that one could play with gold-flecked fish along with a variety of other breathtaking marine life. The beach, however, was my desire, and I was looking forward to sinking my toes into the soft white sand on Seven Mile Beach.

I had hoped to have a few daily excursions into town, but quickly found that most of the pink and yellow shops were of the same nature and lacking in creativity. At first glance the assortment of stores seemed promising, but they were targeted towards the basic tourist and catered heavily to the folks who emerged from the giant cruise boats on a daily basis. Besides beachwear, silver, and diamonds, the most sought after purchases were rum and cake. And yet, the effect on cruise folks was considerably positive, as evidenced by the many shopping bags they toted into the town square.

The resort where I stayed was busy and primarily inhabited by couples and families. It didn't take long for me to realize that there were few men to choose from there—and even fewer in the city. Most men were locals and evidently busy with their choice of employment: taxi driving. It certainly wasn't the best place for finding a potential suitor, but then again, I didn't want to become one of those desperate women drifting from one hotel to the next in search of any man with two legs. There was a brief, painful discerning that I had become someone I didn't want to be—and someone I could easily loathe—but I knew better than to let myself wallow into that kind of state of mind. After two years of healing I was finally coasting, and it was time to lock up the dark thoughts and look forward to the next seven days.

Yet on the third day of my seemingly uneventful holiday, synchronicity found me yet again, this time in Grand Cayman. It was particularly sultry on the day in question, and I entered the elevator that morning only to be startled by a woman's scream from down the hall. As I turned towards the commotion, my only sundress got snagged on a nail and a huge rip tore through the fabric. The woman, it turned out, was only fooling around with her boyfriend, and as they sauntered past me in their own little world of laughter, I stared at them with contempt and envy. They had no way of knowing about my situation or my ripped dress, and yet I somehow expected more from them. *Like an apology.* I held up my dress and stared at the tear, then chastised myself for being so ridiculous as to fall prey to a swarm of self-pity emerging out of nowhere.

A long, low whistle caught my attention and I looked up. "That's a mighty fine rip, darling." A heavyset woman was standing about two feet away. She smelled faintly of honey, and a shiny gold name tag bore the name of Kerida. She was one of the chambermaids, and she was pushing her housekeeping cart towards the elevator. A small lizard scurried away as she gave the cart a strong heave and pushed it into the elevator.

I shuddered at the lizard and smiled at Kerida.

"Go into town to see Araish. She'll find you something nice in no time." Kerida fiddled with a garbage bag as she exited the elevator on the second floor.

"Thanks," I called after her weakly. She disappeared down a narrow corridor and I wondered if she liked her job.

Back in my room, I considered the maid's advice and browsed through a bundle of shop brochures. Right away I saw an ad near the front page of one, and I discovered that Araish owned a small boutique. It was on the Paseo at Camana Bay overlooking a pristine concourse lined with trees and fountains. Interestingly, I recalled taking notice of that same place when I first perused through the hotel's tourist guide. The exquisite fabrics and bold colours seemed to shout out to me from the pages, and for whatever reason, it seemed as if the fates were colluding to get me inside that little shop.

George, the primary concierge at the resort, couldn't have been more helpful. "Missus. Come over here to this silver cabbie. Mr. Max here will take you to the Paseo." Despite the heat, George was dressed from head to toe in a navy suit with brass buttons. As he waved me into the cab with his white gloved hands, he opened the rear passenger door and instructed Max in Jamaican Creole, presumably about my destination. I slid into the backseat, thankful to have a chauffeur, and noticed that he vinyl seats were cracked. Bits of foam were seeping through the seams, and I could smell coconut. Whether it was from an air freshener or from Max's cologne, I couldn't tell. There were a few pictures clipped to Max's sun visor, and I could make out at least four small children. They were obvious reminders of why people like he and George put up with obnoxious tourists day in and day out.

While Max was polite, he was also blessed with a sixth sense that cautioned him to speak only when the situation called for it. As a result, we drove to the Paseo in silence, which was thoroughly appreciated from my end. The open windows let in the ocean breeze, and I was satiated from all directions. The draft felt incredibly good in light of the unbearable heat, and my hair was blowing in every direction. The wind blew my loose white blouse astray, and, in an alluring way, it was like I was being invisibly undressed. I was wearing a lace bra the colour of lavender and I embraced the exposure. I looked down at my arms and couldn't help but notice how the white of my blouse contrasted beautifully with my darkened skin.

I gave Max a handsome tip and walked up the white steps to Araish's Boutique. A beautiful awning offered some immediate shade and the door made a jingling noise as I entered. The scent of fresh freesia immediately swam past me, and the coolness offered by the air conditioner was refreshing. As I attempted to clip my hair into place, I glanced around and saw that Araish, or at least whomever Araish had hired for help, was busy helping another customer. As I turned to inspect a row of colourful dresses, the absolutely unthinkable happened, just like that.

A powerful upheaval turned my world upside down. I think I even sensed that he was there before I saw him. Time was suspended, like the blackness in the room when the film stops running.

He was behind me and took my wrist to turn me towards him. He said my name, and I remember some chatter about the coincidence of finding me here in Grand Cayman, of all places. I think he told me he was working, which would explain his appearance because he was looking more dishevelled than usual. I could tell from the faint trace of dark hair above his upper lip that he hadn't shaved in days, and his hair was longer than I remembered it. He smelled interesting—and not at all like I remembered him. Of course, he was beautiful as always, and perhaps even more so.

Our eyes locked in a trance, and it appeared that nothing could remove the deadbolt that was pulling us together. He was still holding my arm, and then his hand sashayed down my skin to take hold of my hand. He smiled and carefully brushed the hair out of my eyes with his other hand. It was all so surreal. His face was close, and I wanted desperately to kiss him and feel his soft lips against mine. More importantly, his apparent happiness at seeing me seemed genuine.

"Will you ever come back to Lake Huron?" His question caught me off guard, and I had to steady myself on my feet. I was speechless; after all, I had come all this way to get *away* from Jaime Batten, and now here he was, in the last place on earth I'd ever expect to find him. And just as I was about to try to utter some intelligible response, I heard the bell dingle over the front door. I glanced behind him to see a striking black woman stride into the shop. To my astonishment, the local beauty sauntered up behind Jaime and wrapped her arms around his waist, pulling him towards her. She had the most slender arms, I noticed, and I watched in disbelief as she nuzzled her dark lips into his neck and mumbled something about hurrying up. He was still smiling when he turned to look at her. His hand reached up and stroked her face. Was I mistaken, or were they in love?

Everything that followed was a blur. I couldn't be entirely sure, but I recall him taking my hand and asking me where I was staying. I don't think I even answered. He kept telling me that he was working. I seemed to remember him repeating that over and over again. And yet somehow I managed to buy a dress, because when I woke up at four in the morning in my hotel bed, it was crumpled up along with a pile of tissues, soaked with my bewildered tears.

CHAPTER 28

There was a pounding on the hotel door and then my phone was ringing. I was ignoring both until I heard a woman with a strong accent yelling at me to open the door. I was very close to telling her to fuck off before a moment of panic ran through me. What if there was an emergency at the hotel? Were the personnel desperately trying to reach anyone who was ignoring the warnings? I stumbled across the floor, undid the locks, and swung open the door to reveal a plump maid, arms full of toilet paper. She was definitely angry.

"You yell at everyone here last night, and now you no answer your door! That is not nice, Miss Lady. We are not pieces of dried shit here. Who do you think you are?" She barged past me and proceeded to stock the bathroom cupboard with the toilet paper.

I had no recollection of yelling at anyone, but then everything from the previous day had become a blur after four in the afternoon. I had a vague reminiscence that alcohol had been involved. *God, I have to stop drinking.*

The thought of Jaime made me flinch, and then a wave of nausea struck me. I realized that I was either going to be sick or I desperately needed to eat. Luckily, it seemed to be the latter. After the maid left, I took a quick shower and made my way to the poolside café to contend with a severe headache that felt like my brain was splitting in two. I had to tell Emry, the waiter, to leave the pot of coffee at my table. Only after taking a super-strength aspirin could I begin to piece together the events of the day before. Who the hell was that woman with Jaime? Was this part of his undercover job as a cop? Why was he on Grand Cayman, of all places, and why, after almost two years, did I have to meet up with him again? Good Lord, maybe Jaime was married to that local woman! After all, he was often away from Canada for months on end. Maybe I didn't want to entertain this conversation after all. *Here we go again.*

Things had been under control and running somewhat smoothly, and now my life was going to turn upside down again. I wasn't sure I could handle it, especially not here, and the thought of catching a flight back home immediately came to mind. But despite feeling confused and heartbroken, my curiosity was inflamed. I needed information and answers. In particular, I needed to know who that damn woman was. The previous afternoon was a bit of a blur, but I remembered the woman calling out to the shop clerk when she entered. Were they friends? And, most of all, if Jaime was supposed to be gay, why had he looked at and touched that woman the way he had—with obvious desire? I couldn't stand it.

My brain was on fire for the rest of the day as it frantically tried to figure out the riddles that this man brought into my life. So, after I went for a swim in the ocean, I decided to head back into town to speak with the storekeeper. The idea carried its risks, I knew, but it needed to be done. *Does it really need to be done? My oh my, Ann, you are obviously sick.* I commanded my inner voices to shut the hell up as I headed up to my room to get changed for town.

Two hours later, I was standing on the front steps of her store. Again. I paused before entering and was overcome with second thoughts about even being there. But before I could contemplate the thought any further, the shop door swung open in my face. She must have seen me from the window and been anxious to make a sale.

"Hello, honey, you are back. For another dress, I hope?" A deep throaty laugh erupted from her. "Come in. I think I have the perfect one for you." She was a tall, slender woman, almost Amazonian, and yet she walked with the poise of a cat. I followed her into a back corner of the store and she pointed to a two-piece outfit that was indeed gorgeous.

"It's beautiful. May I try it on?" She led me to her makeshift dressing room—a circular hoop suspended from above with draping cotton sheets hanging down—and I contemplated my next words carefully. Thankfully, there was no one else in the store occupying her attention. I had picked a good time to come. "It was so funny yesterday, when I was in your store. I ran into someone from back home… from, um, Canada. I never thought in a million years that I would see him here, of all the places. Can you imagine?"

There was a long pause. I wasn't sure if she had even heard me through the curtain that was dividing us. Then suddenly she pulled away the curtain, startling me. *Everyone certainly is relaxed around here*, I mused, somewhat annoyed. Then I noticed she had a beautiful pair of sandals in her hands.

"Try these on with the outfit." Then she stared at me from top to bottom. "Oh la la, you are one succulent woman."

I could feel myself blushing at her compliment. She turned to stare at my reflection in the mirror. I slipped on the sandals, and indeed, they were marvelous. She certainly had taste.

"And I could see that Mr. Batten thinks so, too," she added.

I pivoted abruptly and stared at her. So she *had* heard what I'd been saying. "What are you talking about?" My blood was on fire.

"I'm talking about the beautiful man who came in here yesterday afternoon. Jaime Batten." She started fussing with her curtains. "He's the friend from Canada you were just talking about, right?"

"I didn't realize he had a girlfriend." I tried to say this with as much indifference as I could muster, but the entire situation was tearing me up inside.

"Yes, but he wants *you*, not her. I could see that plain as day." She gently pulled my hair up from behind, lifting it off my neck. "You need to keep this up when you wear this. It shows off your long, graceful neck. You will look like a beautiful swan. And you will make him even crazier for you."

Crazier? *She* was the crazy one, not him. Worse, this whole situation was crazy. Dare I break the news to her that he was gay? She left the change area, and as I shakily gathered my clothes and redressed, I could feel my heart rate taking on a familiar quick pace—a pace I hadn't felt in a long time. I seriously thought about taking a cab to the airport and going home. *And Renee wonders why I'm nuts? No one else in this universe could have the same bizarre things happen to them*, I seethed.

All of a sudden, she yelled from the register. "Every time he comes to Grand Cayman, the women all want him. He is so beautiful and attentive. His warm heart is rare."

I wasn't sure I could bear being in the store anymore, and I chastised myself for going back there in the first place. *This was stupid, Ann, very stupid.* I approached the register feeling angry, because it seemed like she was making a mockery of me. "He's gay." I said this in a curt way as I firmly placed my purse on the counter. My remark came out like a military command.

A few seconds passed before she began laughing hysterically, which made me even more annoyed. Who the hell was this crazy duck? She either didn't get it, or else she was in on some joke to which I was certainly not privy. I felt like walking out of her store without another word. She could keep her goddamned outfit as far as I was concerned.

She must have registered my sensitivity because she suddenly became serious. She began to wrap my outfit carefully in white tissue, placing fresh freesia within the folds and topping everything off with a gold sticker emblazoned with the store logo. She wrapped the sandals in the same way. Though I was impressed, my cheeks were inflamed with anger. The silence between us was deadly. She delicately handed me my bag and then looked up at me. "Honey, Jaime Batten is not gay. And that's a fact."

CHAPTER 29

Why does the world play nasty tricks on us?

I had withdrawn in forest, and my song
Was swallowed up in leaves that blew away;
And to the forest edge you came one day
(This was my dream) and looked and pondered long,
But did not enter, though the wish was strong:
You shook your pensive head as who should say,
I dare not—too far in his footsteps stray—
He must seek me would he undo the wrong.
Not far, but near, I stood and saw it all
Behind low boughs the trees let down outside;
And the sweet pang it cost me not to call
And tell you that? I saw does still abide.
But 'tis not true that thus I dwelt aloof,
For the wood wakes, and you are here for proof.

I sat at the edge of the ocean, reciting Robert Frost and trying to make sense of all that had happened to me in the last two years. There was a warm breeze that dried my tears. I thought about my divorce, and all the shame and hurt surrounding that. Then my mind turned to my meeting with Jaime, a man who turned my life upside down even though I couldn't have him. *How is life fair?* He was more beautiful than any man I had ever come across, and yet he was gay. Or was he?

My mind began to spin in the same circles it always did. *He's an undercover police officer who is engaged in international affairs that take him beyond our Canadian borders. He is supposedly gay, and yet he almost definitely enjoys the intimate company of women, even though he tells me he is not bisexual. I feel like he's attracted to me, but why does he pull away from me? And a strange local woman tells me he wants me... but does he?*

He was a riddle. *Who is this man?* As I looked out across the aquamarine seas, I questioned who I was, too, and where I was heading. I was a woman who had worked very hard in life and who had carved out a successful professional career, but I was an utter failure when it came to relationships. Worse, I was a dismal wreck when it came to emotions, whether I was receiving them, expressing them, or interpreting them. I felt like a simple woman who was merely asking for the most basic things that life had to offer, and yet I was hoping for the greatest thing on earth—to find a loving relationship with a person who would be my best friend. I ached for someone to grow old with, for someone to love until death did us part. I didn't need extravagance, and I could withstand the complexities, the compromises, and the pain along the way... so long as there was love.

And yet I had somehow trapped myself within a landscape of anxiety and exquisite torture. And just when I'd thought I could finally experience the wonderful feeling of intimacy and togetherness, it was all swept away and replaced by a cold, distant loneliness matched only by the howling ache of the Lake Huron winds.

Despite the warm tropical breezes encircling me, I shuddered.

CHAPTER 30

When Sunday arrived, my bags were packed and I was extremely happy to be going home.

I didn't run into Jaime on the island again, although my mind didn't stop thinking about him for the remainder of my vacation. For the most part I remained sad, and yet I couldn't even define the sadness that was gripping me because it was so abstract.

"Missus, did you enjoy your stay on Grand Cayman?" George was as friendly and courteous as ever, and it was only as I was getting into Max's taxi that I finally took notice of a faint British accent. *I guess everyone has a story brewing just beneath the surface*, I thought.

Max continued to be an absolute delight as he assisted me to the departures drop-off and ensured that all my bags were placed on a trolley inside the airport. "Missus, I hope you enjoyed your stay and will come back to our sunny and friendly shores." He removed his hat and bowed to me. There was a pang in my heart as I thanked him and made my way into the airport. I knew that I would never be making this trip again; it would be too painful.

I passed through security and found a comfortable seat at the far end of my gate. It was midafternoon, and given that I was feeling so depleted, I would have thought that the coincidental appearance of Jaime at the airport would have created some inner surge of energy in me; however, my senses only registered a nominal feeling of surprise as he came into view. In some small way, I suppose I was beginning to get accustomed to the nuances of my life and the effects Jaime had on me.

There he was, standing about twenty feet away. He seemed to have come through a separate door. He was with another man who was wearing a colourful plaid shirt. They looked like the picture-perfect gay couple. *How convenient and appropriate*, I thought as I watched them. They were fiddling with papers, and as I watched, Jaime stuffed a few documents into a type of wallet that he then placed inside his jacket. They looked incredibly serious as they conversed, and both of them looked up frequently and scanned their surroundings. It was like they needed to ensure they weren't being watched, and I debated whether or not I should look away. I chose not to, and of course Jaime registered me immediately the very next time he looked up.

He grinned, which caught me off guard, but I would run with it. I had decided several days ago that I would let fate play out its hand. There was obviously some reason that Jaime and I kept being thrown together, and if I was meant to find out what that reason was, then so be it.

I was tired of being in such a state of immense distress and confusion, and trying to understand the complexities of the situation only made it worse. Over the past few days I had been constantly analyzing and re-engaging myself in every scene or conversation that Jaime and I had shared over the past two years, and nitpicking through the details of these situations until they lost any magic they might once have held. It was killing me, and I needed to let it all go. I couldn't control this time in my life any more than I could control my hair, which had been out of order ever since I'd left Canada. *It's time to give in*, I told myself. As Thea would say, the universe was created in chaos and still exists in chaos. And I was clearly in a state that lacked reason or predictability. Literally, I was in an abyss of confusion.

I tried to recall Ovid's Metamorphoses in my head.

Rather a rude and indigested mass:
A lifeless lump, unfashion'd, and unfram'd,
Of jarring seeds; and justly Chaos nam'd.
No sun was lighted up, the world to view;
No moon did yet her blunted horns renew:
Nor yet was Earth suspended in the sky,
Nor pois'd, did on her own foundations lye:
Nor seas about the shores their arms had thrown;
But earth, and air, and water, were in one.
Thus air was void of light, and earth unstable,

And water's dark abyss unnavigable.

I thought about all of the people who attempt to control their existence as it is, and how, in the end, fate always turns the tables and teaches a required life lesson instead. I was ready to learn my lesson; I was finally willing to let it go.

I looked up to see Jaime walking towards me. He had shaved and was looking rather clean-cut again. I felt all my muscles tighten. It was amazing how my body reacted to this man on an unconscious level.

"Hey, Ann," he said, and then sat down on the seat beside me. It almost seemed like he was relieved to see me, but I stopped kidding myself.

I glanced over to where his partner had been, but he was nowhere to be seen. I crossed my legs and clasped my hands between my knees as I scanned the arrivals and departures screen. It seemed to help with my nerves. He was sitting to my right, and his left arm was hooked around the back of my seat. I decided to stick with the small talk. "Time to go home," I said. *Obviously.*

He quickly glanced at my gate. "I'm on a different plane. We're heading to Washington, and then New York. For work," he clarified. "I'm hoping to be back at the lake sometime in October."

I looked away for a moment. I wondered when his boyfriend would return. I looked back at Jaime, and yet I had nothing to say to him. He seemed to be searching for something in my eyes. It was like he was trying to unearth a mutual understanding, or perhaps communicate a plea of some sort. Did he want my forgiveness for all he'd put me through? *Fat chance, buddy.* I focused on his features to distract me. I could see that his jaw was tense.

"You never answered me in the store when I asked you about coming back to Lake Huron."

I was caught off guard again. I had such a vague recollection of that afternoon and of the conversations that had occurred between us. I had no idea what I may have said while I was so focused on that local woman kissing him. I decided that it was simply safer to be indifferent, so I chose my words carefully. "Oh, I don't know when I'll be back. I'm thinking of maybe selling Heart House." I uncrossed my legs and re-crossed them in the other direction. I was proud of my detachment. Yes, there was the need to throw this information at him and see what became of it, but I looked away because the agony of maintaining eye contact with him was too much.

He obviously did not like it when I broke the connection, because he immediately reached up with his right hand and held my chin, turning my face to look at him. His eyes were serious, dark and intense. His hand dropped to my leg. I could feel his fingers spread out and gently hold my thigh. "Why would you do that?" He looked almost hurt, which surprised me.

Don't fall for it, Ann. This is a dead end, and you know it. "I don't know," I sighed. "It isn't the same at Heart House anymore for me. I'm so busy with work, and I can't write there... and that was the whole idea—a quiet place where I could write."

He glanced at his watch and I became saddened by the fact that this brief yet difficult moment was going to end soon. *Time, please stand still*, I thought.

It was his turn to look away, and when he turned back to face me, I knew he was about to say something that made him uncomfortable. "Is it because of what happened between us?"

Funnily enough, I had rehearsed this exact moment over and over in my endless daydreaming over the past two years. I knew exactly what I wanted to say to this man, and yet the words wouldn't come. I bit my lower lip and actually felt my body start to tremble. *Control, Ann. Get it together.* Suddenly there was an announcement over the loudspeaker. Last call for Washington.

I knew I needed to say the next words as quickly as possible. "Jaime, I was drunk. It was such a silly thing to have happened in the first place. It meant nothing to me. Absolutely *nothing*." My voice was so clear that I surprised even myself. I looked down at my tangled hands and took a deep breath before I spoke again. "We need to forget about that night." For the life of me, I had no idea why I said those words. It was not what I had scripted.

He was very still. He never took his eyes off me as he told me he had to catch his flight. "It's been a long time, Ann. I can't tell you how much it meant for me to see you here in Grand Cayman. I really hope you reconsider selling Heart House." I could have sworn on my mother's life that he looked crushed, yet he said nothing more. He stood up and turned to walk away.

I felt a terrible ache in my chest as I stared at the empty seat beside me. I wondered if I would ever see him again.

CHAPTER 31

The encounter in Grand Cayman forced me to re-evaluate my mental state and finally seek help. Despite my lack of insight and stubbornness, I somehow acknowledged the fact that a trip back to the psychologist was necessary. It was either that or spend Friday nights in the local bookstore's self-help aisle with massive amounts of coffee on hand.

"I want you to stay far away from Jaime Batten. Got it? Think of him like a bug… a sick, putrid insect. Every time you feel the anguish and grief, you need to immediately visualize a loathsome insect that feasts on the dead."

I was sitting on Dr. Harris's cold leather couch, scrutinizing her as she said these words. She wasn't quite five feet tall, and behind her funky green glasses, her eyes were just slightly crossed. Part of me bemoaned the precious dollars I was wasting on this woman, while the other half of me got a carnal satisfaction out of envisioning Jaime as a bug. I hoped that her Pavlovian connection would work.

After ten sessions, I was finally beginning to put Grand Cayman and the images of Jaime behind me. My creative writing juices were beginning to flow again, and the summer was turning out to be better than expected. Renee had convinced me—again—not to sell Heart House, and although she had been successful at renting out the cottage during the previous season, our devoted customers were justifiably disappointed when Renee informed them that Heart House would be closed for business that summer. I was terribly homesick for the sound of the water, and given that Jaime wouldn't be around until October, I had decided that it would be good for me to spend some time at Heart House.

Renee agreed. "Three weeks, honey. No distractions and no renters. It will be just the thing for you. You need it."

So when I finally returned to Lake Huron after two long years, a collective feeling of comfort, strength, and independence embraced me. It felt incredibly wonderful to be so carefree again, and as much as I wanted to adhere to Dr. Harris's advice, I was kidding myself if I didn't admit to casting a few furtive glances towards Jaime's cottage. With the exceptions of the cleaning lady who came every two weeks and Jim who collected his mail, there was absolute silence from Jaime's house.

On the third day of my holidays, I stepped out onto the deck and glanced at my candles, which were warping in the heat. The laughter of small children could be heard in the distance, and immediately I thought of how nice it would be to spend an afternoon at the public family beach for a change. It was only a five-minute walk north on Lake Road, and I always enjoyed the stroll. It gave me the opportunity to potentially meet someone new, to stare at the other cottages, and to admire my neighbours' beautiful hanging plants. The inhabitants of Lake Huron's shores were obsessed with window boxes, and trailing ivy was everywhere.

I gathered my writing materials and packed a light day bag. As I made my way to the beach, I noticed that there was a moderate gale over the water, but not enough to make my papers blow everywhere. The waves were gentle, and the children were full of laughter as they tumbled in and out of the swells. Catamarans and sunfishes were neatly lined up along the edge of the shoreline, and every so often I would witness a group of teenagers pile on a soft canvas tarp and push their regalia out to sea. Their happiness and optimism was contagious, and I was sucking it all in. For the first time in a long time, I was smiling and feeling happy.

Toddlers were playing in the sand and young mothers stood nearby, assisting them when necessary. Older women were still coating oil on their weathered skin, and I appreciated the comfort and confidence they exhibited with their luscious curves spilling over their bathing suit bottoms. The older gentlemen were equally as sun loving and wrinkly, and I couldn't help but chuckle as I watched them lift the lids off their styrofoam coolers to sneak a cold beer when necessary.

After a few hours of writing, I glanced at the teenagers playing a round of volleyball and soon my eyes were darting over to a row of cottages. I blinked a few times as a familiar figure came into view; it was the old gentleman whom I had met at Birch Tree Resort a couple of years ago. He was sitting on a small stump in the shade of a tree, and he appeared to be enjoying the views of the beach as much as I was. He was smoking a pipe and wearing a wide-brimmed straw hat. Within a few minutes he caught sight of me as well, and he waved to me.

I stood up and brushed the sand off my legs before I made my way over to him. "Well, hello there! How are you?" I greeted him, parking myself on the sand in the shade beside him. For the life of me, I couldn't remember his name. It had been too long since I last saw him.

"Delightful, Ann. And you?"

I was mortified that his memory was better than mine. "I'm great." I looked toward the shoreline and watched a boy try to grab a Frisbee, only to drop it and then tumble in the sand. He began laughing hysterically. I smiled and looked back at the old man. "Do you come to the beach often?"

"Sometimes, yes, but the heat can really get to me these days. So I try to stay in the shade as much as I can. I do enjoy the sights and sounds, though, especially those of the children. I really enjoy watching the children. It's good for an old man like me to remember what carefree looks like."

"Does it bring you back to the good old days?" I wanted to steer him back to that conversation we'd started years ago, but I wasn't sure if he would even remember.

"Why, yes it does. Are you referring to my Birch Tree days, Ann?"

I nodded. This man was more astute than I had given him credit for.

He exhaled from his pipe and heaved a deep sigh as he stared out towards the water. "We'd all come down here every single day. I could only come in the evenings, of course, when my shift was over, but the boys and I loved to head out for an evening swim. We'd even do a little fishing if the water was calm."

He proceeded to tell me about some of the history of the Hurons, and for a moment I was reminded of the story Violet had told me about Jaime and the great mystery. I wanted to ask Harold about this, but the opportunity passed as he continued to talk about some of the longstanding families in the region. He also told me about the war and how it changed the lives of so many in the area—particularly his, as he had lost his older brother. He told me that his mother had never been the same after his brother's death; she had died four years after her eldest son had failed to return from Europe.

"What about that Mia girl? Remember, you told me about her? You said how beautiful she was… And what about the fellow named Jaime? Whatever happened with those two?"

I was breaking a Dr. Harris rule, but I didn't care. It was like eating chocolate after a week of dieting. *Bugs be damned.*

"Oh, yes. Jaime and Mia." He took a draw from his pipe, and I watched how he meticulously rolled the smoke around in his mouth before releasing it. I wondered why he was still smoking at this stage in his life. Surely he knew that it wasn't healthy for him. He finally cleared his throat. "The story of the century… at least around these parts. You have a good memory, Ann."

He didn't know the half of it, but I wasn't about to reveal my weakness just yet.

"Jaime was local," the old timer began. As he continued speaking, his name suddenly came to me. *Harold.* Harold McKay. "He was one of the poor chaps, like me, with one parent who was an Indian. For him it was his mother—she was Huron. His father was a Scottish immigrant."

I tried to envision this dark and pale combination.

"So I guess you could say that he was always caught between two worlds, and never felt like he belonged either. I know I never did." Harold stared at the water as he spoke. "The girls sure thought he was handsome, though. Now, I don't know about that, but I do know that he was quiet. Always reading, that one."

A small breeze seemed to come from out of nowhere, and I could see the goose bumps on my skin. "And Mia?" I asked, raising my eyebrows.

"Well, Mia was beautiful, like you." I blushed and looked away. "And Mia loved him dearly. The two of them were a handsome looking couple, but it was not to be."

How ironic, I thought. *A classic crushing love story, not too different from my own.*

Harold busied himself repacking his pipe with tobacco from a little pouch. "You see, Ann, Mia was a Stohm. And Jaime didn't cut into the ranks—the social ranks, that is. Remember, he was part Indian, and back then, that defined everything. So even though Mia loved him, she knew they could never be together."

"Did he want to be with her, though?" I posed it as a rhetorical question, but I needed to hear the answer regardless.

"Well, to tell you the truth, no one was ever quite sure *what* Jaime was thinking." Harold lit a match and brought it up to light his pipe.

He was losing me. I looked at him blankly. "What do you mean?"

"We all thought he was crazy not to be in love with Mia, but he kept his distance. Maybe he knew that she could never truly accept him—as much as she might want to."

I froze for a moment and tried to understand the synchronicity in all of this. Why had I met this old man in the first place? Was this just another twist of fate that was supposed to teach me a lesson? "So, what happened?" Without my noticing it, I had leaned in close to him. The smoke from his pipe was mingling with my hair. "Did she die of a broken heart?" I tried to sound facetious.

Harold turned to look at me. Instead of seeing the expected twinkle in his eye, however, I was aware that he had suddenly become serious. "Ann, do you really think people die of broken hearts?"

His question caught me off guard. I dug my toes into the sand, feeling foolish. "Well, I don't know. People can fall in love, but may not necessarily be able to *be* with the person they love." I paused before I spoke my next words. "It can be very distressing."

Harold smiled with assurance and looked out towards the beach again. When he looked back at me, a small puff of smoke emerged from the corner of his mouth. "Well, I believe that true loves will always find each other. Just keep in mind that the barriers are lessons to be learned."

Was Harold implying that I needed to learn a lesson? "So what happened, Mr. McKay? Did they eventually get together?"

"Well, Mia became pregnant. It was the summer of forty-seven, two years after the war ended. She was seventeen."

I raised my eyebrows. "Really? What about the Stohms? They must not have been too happy about that."

"Furious as can be, actually. And sweet little Mia refused to reveal the name of the father. She attempted to hide the pregnancy as best she could, but she was terribly ill by mid-August and the onsite nurse at the resort confirmed her mother's suspicions."

My interest was piqued. "Obviously Mr. and Mrs. Stohm must have wanted her to get married, particularly in those days?" As distasteful as scandalous stories like this were, I was completely intrigued and wondered where this was heading.

"Oh yes, of course. It was nineteen forty-seven, after all. Times were different then. But there was this little problem of not knowing who the father was, you see. The Birch Tree cottage folks were outraged. Why, poor Mr. Stohm was ready to hang himself with shame, and Mrs. Stohm… Well, she was a mess. She started to frequent the Kincardine apothecary on a regular basis. No one ever knew what she was on, but everyone kept a close eye on her. She had this little black bottle that she snuck from her pocket when she thought no one was looking."

"I'm surprised they didn't pack their bags and head back to Detroit." I twirled circles in the sand with a long stick. "Why did they stay?"

"Well, it was a matter of honour. Mr. Stohm wouldn't leave the resort until the guilty party stepped forward."

Just then a child screamed on the beach and we both turned to look at the commotion. I wondered if the little tyke was tired from too much sun. *Someone should take him in,* I thought. I looked back at Harold and narrowed my eyes. "But she could have gotten pregnant from someone back in Detroit! How on earth could they be sure it happened at Birch Tree?"

Harold adjusted his hat. "Mia was insistent that it happened here. But that was all she'd say."

"Was Jaime the father?" I couldn't help but think about those initials on my tree: MS and JB. In another part of my skull, there was a nagging question as to whether the Jaime in 1947 had a grandson who was named after him. I knew it was far-fetched, but I was going to entertain my theory, if only for a second.

Harold squinted and another puff of smoke came out of his mouth. "Mia swore up and down that Jaime was not the father. But that poor boy looked scared as shit—just like all the other boys that summer."

"So what happened?" The suspense was killing me.

"Well, they left at the end of the summer. Mr. Stohm gave up his crusade to find the father after coming up blank. I can still remember old man Stohm throwing the luggage in the back of his Lincoln and muttering something about the Canadian dirt at Birch Tree Resort. He was referring to us boys, of course."

I decided to speak up. "She was probably every bit as responsible for that outcome as the father was." For some reason, I felt a terrible pang of sadness for Mia despite her wrongdoing.

"Yes, Ann, but you have to remember, it was the nineteen forties. In that era, only us boys were to blame." Harold brushed some sand from the hem of his pants.

"So she had the baby?" I prompted.

Harold nodded. "Yep. A boy. And, you know, she wanted to name that baby Jaime, but her father strictly forbade her."

"So he must have been the father!"

Harold was quick to respond. "No, apparently he wasn't. Mia strongly attested to that, and as it turns out the baby was pale as milk—no sign of any Huron blood in him at all. But I think it was wishful thinking on her part."

"So, who was the father, Harold?" I pressed. Harold pursed his lips. He looked out to the water for several seconds before he turned back to look at me. He cleared his throat.

"She never told," Harold recalled. "There were rumours, of course. One was about the feeble minded janitor, and there was another one about some local boys. There was even talk of her own father being the culprit. But everybody seemed happy enough to pin the blame on the quiet boy, Jaime." He paused again, lost in thought.

"That's terrible." It was all I could think to say.

"Yes, and it gets worse. Mia's mother kicked Mr. Stohm out five months after they'd returned to Detroit, and the following summer, Mrs. Stohm committed suicide. Actually, she did it not far from here. She, Mia, and the baby had stopped at a gas station close to Goderich, and Mrs. Stohm managed to stab herself exactly twenty-nine times in a dirty old outhouse beside the gas bar. Rumour had it that she and Mr. Stohm were married on the twenty-ninth of September, and that was why she stabbed herself so many times."

My jaw fell open. What a sad, sad story. "That's awful!"

"She had been in there a good twenty minutes before someone finally noticed a pool of blood seeping out from under the privy door. Terribly sad, but I guess she just couldn't bear to face the gossip that would befall her at Birch Tree once they arrived."

I tried to picture this terrible tragedy. "Then why on earth would she travel all that way from Detroit, if only to kill herself twenty miles away?" I asked.

Harold cleared his throat again. "Only these shores will ever know the truth. Maybe it was because she knew that Mia needed to be back here. After all her daughter had been through… it was her parting gift to her. But I think she wanted Jaime to be a father to her daughter's baby. At least, that's my theory."

"So she got to see Jaime again?" I asked, hoping against hope that things turned out okay for the two of them.

Harold shook his head. "No. The police took her and the baby back to Detroit immediately. Mia was never the same, of course. Rumour had it that she quickly married a man named Sheffield in Detroit, and then died of a mysterious illness less than a year later." Harold paused for a moment before he uttered his next statement. "Many said she died of a broken heart."

I felt all the blood drain from my face.

He smiled sadly at me and then snuffed out his pipe. "She loved that Jaime, but alas, it never came to be."

I felt like I couldn't feel my extremities anymore. "And what about the child?"

"Well, that Sheffield man couldn't deal with the child. Mia was dead, and with no mother…" Harold trailed off. Nearly a minute passed before he picked up the story again. "The child went to an orphanage. He was named Robert."

Good Lord. What a story. I looked up and realized that the beach was now virtually empty. A cool breeze picked up and I realized that my belongings were still on the beach by the water's edge, and the waves were beginning to crash into the shore. I had become so engrossed in Harold's story that I'd lost track of time.

He slapped his hands against his frail thighs. "Time to go, Ann. It was so nice to see you again. By the way, have you ever heard the song Anniversary Waltz by Johann Strauss?"

I hadn't, and shook my head to let him know.

"They used to play that song every Friday at Birch Tree Resort." He rose from the stump he was sitting on and carefully found sound footing. "I promised my wife that we would dance the waltz for every anniversary that we celebrated."

"And you're still dancing, right?" I grinned, picturing Harold and his wife dancing in some little bungalow not far from there.

It was then that he gently took my hand as we walked across the beach. "Ann, my wife died two years into our marriage. It was cancer. They couldn't save her. I never remarried, but I still play that song every year to remember her, on our anniversary."

I felt a lump form at the back of my throat and was reminded, yet again, that God or some entity was playing a terrible and cruel joke on each and every one of us—on Harold, on Mia and Jaime, on me... And yet, maybe there was meaning to it all. Maybe we were meant to learn that even in the best of times, we can't always have what seems right.

As we walked back towards Harold's cottage, the silence along Lake Road engulfed us. I took the time to admire the red, pink, and purple geraniums that were spilling over from woody containers on a variety of front porches. When we reached Harold's little clapboard cottage, I smiled at the sign that read "1922—The McKays." It was painted in red on a peeling piece of cream-coloured birch. All I could think of was the Anniversary Waltz.

"Harold? Whatever happened to Jaime? Did you ever remember his last name?"

"Well, my dear," he said, looking up the road to the south and squinting. "He stayed here, of course. He stayed on the Huron shores."

I followed his eyes and his gaze to the south. My heart started beating faster, but I didn't know why. My question came out in a tight whisper. "Is he still here? Is he still alive?" I couldn't believe how consumed I was by this story.

Harold retrieved a small paper bag from his window sill and began throwing peanuts onto a small path leading from his front door. I wondered if the peanuts were for the chipmunks.

"Harold?"

"Oh yes, he's still alive. He's an old man now, of course, like me. He's living in a nursing home in Kincardine. He had a place down the road, but he's in the home now." Harold was reaching for a bag of seed for the birds. He was beginning to look tired, and I felt guilty for demanding that he continue to tell me about this story. Yet I couldn't walk away without knowing the truth. Poor Mia. She'd died of a broken heart, and by sheer coincidence, that was what was going to happen to me, too; I felt sure of it. Maybe meeting Harold was a sort of cosmic warning—a last chance for me to set things right.

I was afraid to ask the dreaded question, but there were far too many mysteries here and I was afraid of never sleeping again if I didn't get some answers. "Did he, uh, have children? Get married? Does he have any grandchildren, by chance?"

Harold, who had been throwing the seed for the birds, immediately stilled. There was a moment of hesitation, and then he carefully laid the bag of seed on the window shelf and moved to sit down on the bench that was beside his side door. He was looking terribly old and tired all of a sudden.

I sat down, too, even though I was certain that he was growing tired of me now. "What about children?" I pressed. "Did he have any?"

"Oh, yes, there was the boy." His voice was getting weak with fatigue. Maybe he'd missed his afternoon nap, or perhaps we had spoken too much.

"What do you mean, the boy? What boy? Who was his wife?" My voice became intense. I got up and began to pace on his porch.

Harold sighed heavily and closed his eyes. "Ann, there was no wife."

No wife? How could there be no wife, especially back then? It would have been unheard of for a man to raise a child on his own. This was crazy.

Harold spoke again. "It was all so strange, because around the time that Mia died, either just before or just after, Jaime disappeared for a while. And then he was back in Kincardine with the baby." Harold kept his eyes closed, but a smile was tugging at his mouth. "It was Mia's boy, Robert, and son of a gun, he was the cutest kid on earth." Harold began chuckling in earnest now.

What? Jaime raised Mia's son here on Huron shores?

"Why, I remember when Jaime brought him to work at the Birch," Harold continued. "He had the most devilish smile. And such a twinkle in his eye! All the maids would swoon over him and buy him whatever he wanted at the tuck shop. Oh yes, that boy was a delight."

I had to ask the question. There were just too many similarities. "Harold? Do you think it was Mia and Jaime's child? I mean, why else would Jaime go all that distance to track down a child that wasn't his and adopt him from the orphanage?"

"Well, no, we never thought that Jaime was the father. After all, he was such a quiet boy. and he would never do that to Mia—get her pregnant and then deny it, I mean. He was a good man. An *honest* man."

None of this made any sense. I wondered if Harold knew more than he was telling. Maybe he didn't want to speculate about the past indiscretions of a man who, by all accounts, was still very much alive in a Kincardine nursing home. I turned to look at Lake Huron and became mesmerized for a long time. The sun was setting and the breeze was picking up. "Where did old man Jaime live before he moved to the nursing home? You said something about him living just down the road? Did you ever remember his surname?"

There was no answer, so I turned to face Harold. I could see that he was dozing off, so I touched his arm lightly, which startled him.

"Harold, where did the old Jaime live before he went to the nursing home? You said he was down the road from here?"

"Oh, let me think," he murmured, sleep pulling on him again. "I'm not sure what the number would have been… Maybe…" He mumbled something that I couldn't quite catch.

What did he say? Thirty-six Lake? Three thirty-six? Three sixty-six? "And his last name? Did you ever remember his last name?"

But Harold was softly snoring now. I got up quietly and began my lonely walk home.

CHAPTER 32

There is something to be said for events that happen in life that repeat themselves over and over again. Cyclical dramas that need to be played out until some sort of truth is revealed, regardless of time or space. They pay heed to the metaphysical level of our world, or perhaps to our existence, reaching out to innocent bystanders and hoping that past wrongs can be made right. Do we live in a universe where causality and possibility are intertwined and interrelated, yet potently discreet to the human eye?

My fingers hovered over the laptop keyboard. Since my conversation with Harold, synchronicity was the only thing I could write about. The story of Mia and Jaime was from a different time, yet the underpinnings were frighteningly similar to my own inherent conflict. This was compounded by my crude recall of the initials carved on the tree outside my cottage. MS and JB… I couldn't help but think that the old Jaime's last name had been Batten, too, and that MS was Mia Stohm, the woman he loved so much that he traveled to another country to save her son from being raised parentless. I slammed my laptop shut.

Everything was too mysterious, and the irony of having two men named Jaime in this area dumbfounded me. Jaime's parents had died, I knew that, but there was the question of the old man in the nursing home. And whatever became of Robert? There was no further mention of him by Harold. Ridiculous as it was, I needed answers—and I needed the Internet. And when the dial-up connection didn't cooperate in my little cottage, I had no choice but to get in my car and drive for ten minutes until I was able to pick up some unsecured wireless signal from someone's farm house.

The moon was bright and the crickets chirped endlessly as I parked my car on the side of the road and tried to find as much information as I could about Birch Tree Resort. There were copies of old newsletters online, and as I scanned the names that were listed, I wished fervently that Harold had revealed old Jaime's last name to me. I came across the Stohm name, but nothing of great interest came of it. I couldn't even find anything listing the employees.

Out of curiosity, I typed 'Jaime Batten' into Google to see what would come up. Interestingly, there was a child welfare case from 1996 in Newfoundland, and although I queried this for a second, I realized that it had to be a different Jaime, as the Jaime I knew would have been too old at that time to be a child of the state. There were other entries, but nothing of interest. The name was just too common, and despite scanning and clicking on a number of links, the information led to nothing.

I was beginning to feel tired and somewhat frightened on this barren stretch of highway, but just as I was about to log off, my eyes glanced at an obituary at the bottom of the screen. I double clicked. The information had been printed in the Kincardine Independent. *Lucille (Pollack-McKee) Batten, formerly of Tiverton, and Robert Batten, of Inverhuron, died at the Kincardine and District General Hospital on Thursday, Nov. 5, 1995 following a sudden and tragic accident at their home. Dearest daughter of the late Bernice and Thomas Pollack; son of Jaime Batten (senior), and mother and father of Jaime Batten (junior); pre-deceased by Lucille's daughter Louise McKee. Private arrangements for funeral and cremation to follow in Tiverton.*

So the old Jaime's last name *was* Batten… and Mia's son Robert *was* my neighbour's father! They *were* related. I immediately remembered those words I heard at the party. *Tragic past.*

It was at that moment that I slammed my laptop closed and hit the accelerator, hard. There was something about this whole thing that was warning me to get away, and fast.

CHAPTER 33

I packed my bags on Sunday afternoon and decided that I was done with Lake Huron, Kincardine, and Lake Road. I loved the beauty of this country, and yet it felt haunted all the same. I could not fathom how the adventures of the last three years had led me to this crazy existence, and although I tried to rationalize every little point in my journey, nothing made any sense at all. There were too many coincidences, synchronicities, and things that went bump in the night. I began to feel like my life had been carved out in advance and there was no turning back and no turning forward—just continuous curve balls being thrown at me from every angle. It wasn't fair, because I had never asked for this.

I even considered that maybe the water was contaminated up here. Perhaps it was the magnetic resonance of the wind mills that made people do crazy things like fall in love with the wrong people? It was like love and pathology existed in tandem on these shores. Like Mia and I; we were one and one alike. We were both in love with men—Jaime Batten Senior and Jaime Batten Junior, to be exact—who were within reach, but impossible to have.

I was inclined to think that the senior Jaime Batten was the biological father of Robert Batten. Why else would he have travelled all the way to Detroit to adopt some illegitimate child, unless it was his own? No one in their right mind would do that unless they had some vested interest. But then again, maybe he'd done it because he really had loved her. Or had he? Other than a pair of carved initials on a tree, did I really have any evidence of this assumption? And what about Robert? Obviously, he was the biological father of *my* Jaime but who was Jaime's mother? I thought back to my conversation with Jim on that warm sunny day. Didn't he say something about Jaime's step-mother? Was *Lucille* Jaime's biological mother?

My sister, Thea, would say that perhaps I was Mia. A reincarnate, of all things, brought back in this lifetime to obtain a second chance at the love she'd been unable to obtain the first time. I actually dwelled on this thought for a moment, and wondered if perhaps it could be true.

And yet, at the same time, I knew it couldn't be true. The reality was more likely that Jaime—*my* Jaime, if I could even consider him that—was just a mysterious man who was perhaps intrigued by me, his love-crazed neighbour. And besides, there was still the question of his sexuality.

I began locking the doors and closing all of the windows in Heart House. I cleaned thoroughly, because I knew that I would be meeting with Renee in Toronto to make a final decision about selling this place once and for all. I managed to do all this despite a throbbing headache and countless tears. When my bags were stuffed in the car, I slammed the trunk and locked the front door, watching in silence as the wooden heart swung gently from side to side. I was filled with longing as I thought of the symbolism around this tiny little piece of wood.

Throughout the drive home, I thought about Mia and her pain—*our* pain. I thought about the senior Jaime Batten and pictured him travelling all the way to Detroit to see her in 1948. I could almost feel his angst as he tried to track her down. I envisioned that he really had loved her, and perhaps they'd had a beautiful reunion filled with desire and pain before she'd finally passed away. At least, I *hoped* she'd gotten to see him one last time.

As the city lights drew nearer, a faint melody could be heard from my speakers and I turned the radio up. It was a lovely tune. When it was finished playing the announcer said that it was the Anniversary Waltz. Clearly, I wasn't going to be able to get away from this mystery, no matter how hard I tried.

CHAPTER 34

Once I was back in the city, my research was thorough.

I couldn't sleep for many nights and spent every moment on the Internet, searching and scanning. I made another visit to Kincardine, where I stalked people and asked questions. Many questions.

I was able to learn that Jaime Batten Senior had remained a single man, but had lived for the joy of his son Robert and his eventual grandson, Jaime Junior. So when Robert died in the tragic house fire in 1995 at the age of forty-seven, the other half of Jaime Batter Senior's world had finally fallen along with Mia. It had been too much for him to bear, and so the old man had sought refuge and solitude within the confines of his cottage. He had loved animals and spent endless hours carving the tiniest versions from bits of spruce and poplar.

Now, a few weeks after Harold told me the story, I had finally gathered up enough courage to venture out to three sixty-six Lake Road, where I found a sanctuary of figurines. They lay everywhere, on each windowsill and doorstep, an homage to things loved and lost. Miraculously, although somewhat dirty, buried, or overturned, they had survived every winter.

They seemed to be protecting his home, like they were waiting for him to come back.

Jaime Batten Senior had only his grandson left—the Jaime I knew. What I found most interesting was that the younger Jaime's biological mother was *not*, in fact, Lucille. According to my research, the woman who brought Jaime—*my* Jaime—into this world would never be known. For whatever reason, Robert Batten had kept this a secret, and it had remained a mystery ever since.

I peered through the old windows of Jaime Senior's cottage and could make out some pictures on the fireplace mantle. One was a framed photo of an attractive woman; I could only assume it was Mia. Beside it was a photo of a young boy who appeared to be about eleven years old. Definite traces of Mia were on his face. It must have been Robert. He was smiling and looking extremely proud as he stood on the shores of Lake Huron.

At least three generations of Batten men had played on the shores of Lake Huron. Robert had lived with his adopted father Jaime Senior in this small cabin, and then reared the younger Jaime as a single parent. I had learned through my incessant questioning that Robert had carried on the tradition of working at Birch Tree Resort like his father. There had been long hazy summer days spent fishing, and the locals recalled how on occasion the elder Jaime could be spotted from the Queen Street Bridge, carefully choosing a lure for the younger Jaime. They would both be kneeling on the rickety dock facing the Seguin River, carefully searching the waters for spotted trout or the occasional pike that was travelling with the current. They were quiet and contemplative, but forgiving.

The three generations of Battens volunteered whenever they could and helped out with local events when needed. Robert even learned to play the bagpipes and took part in the weekly Scottish parade. It was said that during one such Saturday evening, the younger Jaime was hoisted atop a police cruiser by a constable named Mark Barns—the same Mr. Barns who had owned Heart House before me—and from that day forward, Jaime had never looked back from his dream of entering the police force. Robert and Mark had met as youngsters, and continued to have a worthwhile friendship well into their adult years. In fact, it was Mark Barns' wife who had introduced Robert to Lucille. And, of course, this led to the purchase of neighbouring properties years later. *Our properties.... Jaime's and mine.*

The younger Jaime had lived with his father and step-mother Louise on their newly purchased property, but he'd spent equal amounts of time with his grandfather down the road. It was said that he treasured every moment he could have with his grandfather, almost as much as he did the time he spent with his parents. After Robert and Lucille died in 1995, young Jaime made the difficult decision to leave Lake Huron's shores. He was nineteen years old and was intent on pursuing his police career.

Old Mr. Batten was alone, yet again.

CHAPTER 35

Time went on, and as the September sun sank lower in the sky, a lingering feeling of despondency suffocated me. It was a terrible feeling of hopelessness bound up with sadness.

Surprisingly, Renee tried very hard to convince me not to sell. Her brilliant arguments came from every imaginable angle, from the beauty of the environment to a fairly convincing rendition of her dogged determination to find that cottage in the first place. And now, it would all have been for nothing—her words, not mine. At least she had the decency to keep Jaime out of the discussion. Trying not to think about him was challenging, especially since I still had so many unanswered questions. But I knew that the best remedy was to put it all behind me and try to start fresh again.

How many times have I said that before? I chuckled to myself as I recalled trying to do just that when destiny had placed Jaime in the same tourist shop right alongside me, hundreds of miles from home. I guess I sort of figured that destiny would keep this ball in the air somehow—at least for a while.

So when the phone rang one Thursday evening when I was back in Toronto and Renee told me she had an offer on Heart House, I was speechless—not to mention surprised that fate would move in on me so quickly.

"Do I need to go up there to sign papers or something?" I felt myself stretching for any possible excuse to visit Heart House just one more time. I wanted to see him, to say goodbye. It was already the middle of September and he'd said he'd be returning in October.

"Darling." God, I could recognize that condescending tone anywhere. "We're not in the dark ages anymore. There are such things as computers, email, and Blackberries."

"I just thought that maybe they needed original signatures or something." I felt stupid, knowing that Renee could read me like a book. I hurried to change the subject. "Who are these people, anyways? Did you meet them?"

"I don't know. This is very private as I understand it."

I thought about Jaime and how he'd wanted Heart House in the first place. I wondered if he was the buyer. *Dare I ask?* "Do you know if Jaime is buying it?"

Renee sighed. "I don't know, Ann, but I'm almost certain he isn't."

"Really? How?"

"He's not in the country, remember?"

Suddenly a disturbing memory entered my head: dark lips on his sinewy neck. I shook my head to get the picture out of my mind. He certainly had been gone for a very long time. "Yes, of course. But he could still be buying it, couldn't he? Didn't you just say that you could buy and sell anything from anywhere?"

"Why do you care, anyways?" Her abrupt question caught me off guard, and I didn't say another word. That terrible sad feeling hit me again, and it was smothering me.

"I don't." It was only a whisper, but I was certain she heard it.

CHAPTER 36

Four weeks later, the leaves were blowing across Lake Road and yellow and crimson mums were beginning to replace the dying impatiens still hanging in half-dead droves from the cottages' window boxes. It was early October, and dusk. *Why did you come back here, Ann?* I chastised myself. *You are your own worst enemy, you know.*

It was more difficult than I had imagined when I came upon Heart House. It pained me to think that I couldn't walk on the property without feeling like I was trespassing. I stole some glances in the direction of Jaime's house, but there was no car or truck in the driveway. His lights were out and I could only surmise that he was still out of the country. I glanced at Heart House and saw two cars parked in my former driveway. The license plates were yellow and from Maryland. *So they're American.*

I parked my car along the side of Lake Road and walked towards the beach. For whatever reason, I needed to hear the water one last time and feel the cool sand under my feet. God, how I had missed this beach, and now I would never again be able to enjoy it like I used to. What had I done? I could feel the sting of tears mixing with the brisk October wind off Lake Huron, and an empty feeling consumed me.

I pulled my sweater close around me as I walked towards the water. The beach was completely deserted and the sound, as always, was music to my ears. It took a while, but eventually the wind let up and a peaceful calm came over both the beach and me. Darkness was setting in fast, and as I looked north, I caught sight of a bonfire flickering in the distance. So there was someone else out there, too. *Probably wallowing in sorrow like me*, I thought.

I began to walk along the edge of the water, staring at the shells and pebbles that had washed up on the shore. The water was lapping at the shore in perfect rhythm. It was then that I noticed the shadow of a figure sitting close to the water's edge a short distance in front of me. I stopped in my tracks for fear of intruding upon this person's privacy. He or she was alone, and I wanted to respect their solitude. I turned to walk away, but just as I was about to take my third step, he called out to me. I couldn't bring myself to turn around. *God, is it really him? How can this be happening?*

"Ann!"

I could hear his feet splashing through the water as he came towards me. I still didn't turn around, but knew he was close. All at once, his hand took my arm from behind. It was incredible how his touch still felt like electricity to me. I thought I was going to cry. I wasn't sure if it was due to happiness or sadness or a combination of both.

"Ann! Turn around, for God's sake. It's me—Jaime." He was slightly out of breath.

I turned around and almost stopped breathing as I came face to face with the same beautiful features I had first admired several years ago. I could barely speak. The wind picked up and my voice went hoarse. "Jaime! You startled me. I didn't think anyone else was on the beach."

He reached up and tenderly brushed the hair from my eyes. His eyebrows came close together as he scrutinized my face. There was a distinct trace of shadow above his lip and along the edge of his jaw. "Why did you sell Heart House?" He looked hurt and sad, and I knew it was genuine. "I thought you loved it up here. What about the writing?" His right hand slid down to mine. It was dry and warm to the touch.

With extreme bewilderment suffocating me, I wasn't sure what to say. How could this man not know that he had broken my heart, and it was for only this reason that I had to sell?

"Will you come back and sit with me? I've got a fire going." He gestured up the beach, but even as he did so, he seemed tense. I could feel it just as much as I could feel the wind on my face.

My heart rate began to increase and I became nervous. *Ann, he's gay, remember?* I tried to talk my heart down from the heights it was beginning to climb, but I simply couldn't. I nodded weakly and we started towards the flickering flames. He never let go of my hand and pulled me close beside him as we made our way across the beach. A full moon was rising over the lake, and other than the sound of the waves and the sand crunching beneath our feet, nothing more could be heard. The brisk October cold was also settling in, and as we walked in silence, shivers ran through me.

I could concentrate only on the feel of his smooth fingers next to mine. He held my hand firmly, and I detected that something wasn't quite right. We reached his small fire and sat down on a flannel blanket that was laid out beside it. The flames were blowing away from us, but the heat of the fire was urgent and inviting. My skin immediately began to regain some of its lost warmth. I pulled my knees up close to my chest and rested my chin on top. The moon looked huge and orange as it hung low over the horizon.

I stretched out my legs. Jaime eased himself down on the blanket and lay on his side and I could feel just how close to me he was. He reached over and took my hand in his again, carefully toying with my fingers. A few moments passed before he spoke. "I'm a really mixed up fellow, Ann. You don't know the half of it." I knew he was staring at me but I found it hard to return his gaze. "My job requires me to assume various identities. And sometimes, when I'm home, I need to keep things in check because I never really know who could be watching me. Even here, in this very small town of Kincardine."

I was trying to understand where this conversation was heading; it was all so muddled and confusing. All the same, my heart was racing.

"I can't trust people right away, Ann. Sometimes it takes a long time for me to trust someone new." He adjusted his position and moved closer to me just as the light from the fire started to flicker faster in the wind. There was a long pause and then he sighed. "I'm afraid you're going to be really upset with me for saying this." I braced myself for what was coming. He seemed unsure of whether to continue. He finally cleared his throat. "I'm not gay, Ann, and I'm truly sorry for telling you that." He reached up and stroked my face. His hand came back down and took my hand again.

I was experiencing a flurry of emotions. My heart was beating madly and I wasn't sure if I was supposed to be elated with this news or angry. I continued to stare at the lake.

"It was part of an identity I had to assume for work. It was all part of a larger scheme that took me to California, Italy, and eventually to the islands. Sometimes it's easy for me to try to get lost in these different identities that I take on… I guess I try to escape into them when things in my real life get too tough. I know that must sound strange, but it's true." He squeezed my hand. "It wasn't right what I did to you, Ann. Anyone in Kincardine could easily have told you otherwise."

I looked down at the blanket but I knew he was still watching me. *You are such a fool, Ann.*

"It was a major drug bust, Ann, but it's over now. Can you please look at me?"

I slowly turned to look at him and saw how his beautiful blue eyes were searching my face for forgiveness. I didn't know what to say as the last three years flashed by me in pieces.

"Ann… my life is difficult with this job. The travelling, the discretion… Do you understand?"

I didn't.

"Oh, God, Ann." He sighed and rolled over onto his back. "I'm still not being completely honest with you. There is so much more to this that you don't know." His hands came to his face and he rubbed his eyes.

What on earth does he mean by that? I lowered myself to lie on the blanket beside him and stared up at the stars, silently asking for answers. The air was cool, and yet I wasn't cold. The sheer quiet of the night was soothing, and I was content to just lie there beside him without any words.

A few minutes passed in silence, and then he turned towards me. His warm arm came over me and pulled me slowly towards him. There was a brief moment of hesitation, and then he placed his lips on mine. It was a small kiss, and then he let go of me. He brushed more hair away from my face and stroked my cheek. "I think you're so beautiful, Ann."

I felt myself blushing, but before I had time to utter some clumsy response, I felt his hand deftly slide under my hair and behind my neck as he brought me towards him once again. He was hungry, and I could feel his urgency. His other hand reached underneath my waist, pulling my body closer to him, and I could detect a desperate yearning coming from him. As his lips left my mouth and moved across my cheek, he whispered the words I had waited to hear for three long years.

"I want you Ann."

He was in full control, and that scared me somewhat. His hands grazed over me with gentle assurance and I shuddered as he moved them away from my face and down my body. Beneath my light shirt my senses were on fire, and a gnawing ache was suddenly present between my legs.

Our chemistry was intense, and I eventually became comfortable with my own exploration. I began at his broad shoulder, and my fingers gently felt his hardened muscles running along his neck and chest. As I moved my hand along his hard stomach, he began to kiss me more forcefully. The dance of ecstasy had begun as our hands moved endlessly with the sheer need of wanting and needing so badly. He gently pushed me on my back and moved in on top of me. My hand reached his hip and I pushed him against me. He groaned and the fact that I could influence this pushed me even further beyond my comfort zone. I wanted to do more for him. I wanted to give him everything.

My lips passed over his skin and my mouth drew in his scent just as he began to slowly undress me. The cool air felt wonderful on my exposed skin, and my body responded in unison. He came back to kiss me as his warm hands warmed my skin and carefully positioned me beneath him. He was ever so delicate and his touch felt so good that I began to feel delirious. I had never felt so beautiful as I did at that moment. When he moved away from my mouth and I felt his tongue trail across my chest, I knew that we'd found a mutual taste of exquisite love. I pulled gently on his belt, letting him know that I wanted more.

"Are you sure, Ann? Because I don't think I'd be able to stop if…"

I reached down and felt everything. And then I raised my hips into him once more. He took my cue and lay back on top of me and my arms reached around his neck to bring him closer. My lips drew him in again, and he tasted incredible—just like he had that night by the trees. This time, however, nothing would come between us. I felt an incredible surge of joy at just knowing that.

I marvelled at the large dark shadow that was hovering over me and I could feel a primordial, distant tingle as he stirred up a buried need. I reached down and took hold of him. He let out a loud groan as I clasped my hand tightly. He felt incredible.

I let go and he moved closer to me. I felt a faint shudder as our bodies came together and he became a part of me. He pushed deep inside and I felt complete. I wanted all of him within me. Forever.

There was a beautiful symmetry to our movement that gradually built, and just when I thought I couldn't bear it any longer, there was a tremendous release as my core gave way to the dark heavens above. I granted him everything I had before his own body bequeathed its existence to the stars. When he wrapped his whole body around me and we gazed at the moon, I gave a tiny sigh of contentment.

We walked in silence back to his cottage several hours later. I went ahead upstairs, and had only just nestled into his bed when I saw his shadow in the doorway. I wasn't timid this time as he moved towards the bed to join me. We had intermittent moments of sleep throughout the night, but we couldn't get enough of each other. As the night progressed he became careful and methodical, like a cat seeking its prey. He took great care to touch, explore, and satisfy me, and I tried to do the same for him. Our bodies were working in unison, needing and wanting with a purpose. There was a beautiful fluency to everything we did—almost as if we had done this before.

But there was a nagging feeling at the back of my mind, just behind the veil of my consciousness. We were being threatened by the loss of this moment.

It honestly felt like time was running out.

CHAPTER 37

I was met with a lazy, hazy feeling upon waking the next morning, for I had been in an extreme delusory state, almost paralytic, or perhaps catatonic.

I rolled over in the bed, only to realize that the space next to me was empty. My head lay like a dead weight on the pillow while my hand felt for warm skin. There was none to be found. It took a moment before things registered, but eventually I propped myself up on my forearms and realized he was not in bed with me.

It was very quiet in the house. The sheets slipped away from me and I smiled as I recalled how he had touched me. He had done this in such a beautiful way that he had driven me to madness. I rolled over on my back and yearned for him.

Where was he?

***

Dear Ann,

I am sorry to have left you so quickly, but you were sleeping like an angel this morning and I couldn't bear to wake you. Thank you for such a beautiful night. I will never forget it.

I wanted to tell you that I was required to be up before dawn because I am scheduled to be in Vancouver by end of day today. Things progressed quickly between us last night, and there wasn't much room for a conversation; otherwise, I would have told you beforehand. I'm sorry.

I will be away for several weeks. I wish I could contact you, but I can't. I will explain later. The time will go by quickly, so let's not think about it. In the meantime, stay as long as you like. The spare key is in the mailbox. I will be back on Christmas Eve, and I hope that you and I can spend Christmas together at my place. I will wait for you on Christmas Day here on Lake Huron. There is so much to explain.

Again, I am so sorry about this. I will be thinking of you constantly.

Jaime

xo xo

After I read the note he left for me on the kitchen island, I panicked momentarily. Then I remembered that I knew I could trust him.

With the exception of a clock ticking in the background, the silence surrounding me in his kitchen that day was deafening, and there was an unmistakable fog that cast me adrift. I called Renee on my cell phone immediately. My hands were shaking. She knew something was up because I never called her so early in the morning.

"Ann? Are you okay?"

"I'm fine, Renee." My voice was different and she must have sensed it.

"What is going on? Are you hurt?"

"I'm not hurt. In fact, I'm elated. I ran into Jaime last night." My voice was teasing as I played a brief rendition of the past night in my head again.

"You have got to be kidding me. What the hell happened?"

"Well…" I couldn't find the words. I still couldn't believe it myself. "We… uh, we…"

"Ann." She had that adamant and serious tone in her voice. I waited for a few seconds before the magic words were revealed as I nibbled on my fingers. "We slept together."

There was a long, silent pause.

"Yes, Renee. With him. Jaime." The giddiness in my voice was apparent.

She still hadn't said anything.

"Renee?"

"Are you absolutely fucking kidding me? What the hell? I thought he was gay! Jesus."

She didn't sound very excited, and as I waited for her response, worry began to overcome me. I knew she was going to say something that I wouldn't necessarily like. "Ann, you know he might have just used you, right? Some gay men are like that. They just need a quick fix, but men will always come first. You know that, right?"

Now it was my turn not to respond. Why did she always have to spoil things?

"Ann?" She raised her voice.

"It's not like that, Renee. First of all, gay men don't do that, and second of all, Jaime is not gay. I can say that with almost one hundred percent certainty after the night we had together. We spoke about it. You see, he needs to create this facade with respect to his job."

All I could hear was Renee's breathing.

I forged on. "He had to leave again, but apparently he has quite a bit to explain to me. I know there's a story behind the gay front. Do you know what I'm saying? It's his line of work. He's an undercover detective, remember?"

The silence was beginning to bother me.

"Renee," I pleaded—and I hated pleading with Renee. "Look, I know what I know, okay? And there *is* something there." I emphasized 'is,' but even as I said the words, I began to question it myself. "He left me a note before he left. It's beautiful."

More silence. *Damn you, Renee.*

"Renee? What the hell? Are you there?"

"I'm here."

"You're so quiet. It's not like you. Can you at least say *something*?"

"I don't know what to say, Ann. Something's not right with this guy… He lies about being gay, and then he sleeps with you and takes off in the morning? It doesn't make any sense. I'm worried about you."

"Renee, I'm fine, okay? Stop worrying."

And that was the end of our conversation. A stilted, abrupt, and awkward dialogue marred by my own feelings of insecurity, fear, and unease.

Damn you. Damn you, Renee.

***

The feeling was definitely creepy—or, at least, that is how I recall it. I stayed at Jaime's for the remainder of the weekend, and it just so happened that while I was exploring his second-floor bedrooms the next day, my eyes suddenly caught sight of Harold standing in the laneway in front of the cottage. He was standing very still and leaning on his cane. He almost seemed possessed as he stared at Jaime's cottage. He looked to be more unstable with his balance today, for he nearly toppled over when he raised a hand to adjust his cap over his ears. His eyes never left the cottage.

Although I debated going out and speaking to him, I couldn't shake the creepy feeling brought on by watching him. This was not the same sweet man I had spent the afternoon on the beach with a couple of months ago. As I peered through the blinds, I could see that he was tense and that something, indeed, was bothering him.

After a few minutes, his lips began moving. *Is he chanting?* It was at that moment that I stepped back from the window and retreated a few feet back. Harold McKay was, for all I knew, a lovely old man, but his current behaviour had definitely taken me by surprise.

Why on earth was he chanting?

The Harold McKay incident took hold of me for many days. I returned to the city in a mild state of distress. I kept picturing Harold in the laneway, and I'd get goose bumps every time. *Give him a break, Ann*, I reasoned. *He lives alone, and there's a possibility that he's beginning to deteriorate with age.* And yet, he had been so alert and oriented in the summer when we had last spoken.

I also couldn't get Jaime out of my head. I missed him terribly, and I frequently wondered if he was experiencing a similar agony on his part. I hated that I couldn't even call him. There were nights when I would roll onto my side and reach out to touch him, only to discover that he wasn't there at all, and that my hand was searching vainly in the dark air beside me. On those occasions I would lie still in my disoriented state and try to recreate our night together from beginning to end, and somehow this would enable me to fall back asleep again.

I had difficulty concentrating at work, and I spent long minutes staring at the calendar, counting each day up to and including his return. And when I wasn't counting, I would daydream about how we would spend the Christmas holiday, or try to imagine our future, including trips around the world and long hours in bed. The work was piling up on my desk, but I just sat there, starry eyed and motionless, day after day.

Two weeks later, my disoriented mindset was rudely interrupted when Renee called. She was panting and I knew that she was on the elliptical at her club. She had a longstanding habit of phoning personal and business acquaintances while in a sweat-crazed state. Apparently it made her think more clearly.

"Listen, Ann, I got a call from the new owners of Heart House. Apparently, some old man keeps walking over to Jaime's place, and he just stands there on the road. Every time they go out to speak with him, he gets angry and yells out the words 'shame' or 'Huron shame' or something like that. Did this happen when you were there? The owners were going to call the police, but they thought they'd check with me first in case I knew anything about it. I convinced them to hold off on calling the cops until I talked to you."

Huron shame? I felt a twinge of sympathy for Harold. He had definitely lost his mind.

"His name is Harold McKay." I felt like I was condemning him. "I met him some time ago, and he really is a lovely man. But I saw him do the same thing once, and to tell you the truth, it *was* sort of creepy. I can only guess that he's losing his senses given his age. Maybe someone should follow up with a doctor."

Renee spoke up. "Maybe they can try and speak with his neighbour or something, although I think they're heading back to Maryland at the end of the week. Whatever… If he's nuts, they can just ignore it, I guess."

Renee's approach didn't surprise me. Call him nuts and leave him to rot in the dust. *Very thoughtful, Renee.*

We chatted for another fifteen minutes. When I placed the receiver back in its cradle, I thought long and hard about Harold. He was living alone, and he had no one. If he was having some sort of health crisis, perhaps there was no one to help him. I contemplated the situation for the next hour before finally coming to a decision that, by all accounts, could have been interpreted as downright crazy. But I felt that I had no other choice.

It was three in the afternoon. I glanced at the piles of work on my desk and sighed. *Someone's got to do it*, I reasoned, *and it's not like anything will get done around here anyways.*

CHAPTER 39

November turned out to be so cold and gray that people were already cringing and complaining at the mere thought of winter approaching. Miserable folks could be seen turning up their collars, coughing into their sleeves, and scurrying from their cars into warm, heated buildings. And yet the crisp, frosted grass that laced the roads and countryside provided a peaceful reprieve.

It was the day after Renee had called me and I had been knocking at Harold's door for almost ten minutes with no response. I'd even tried to look in some of the windows, but the shades were drawn and it was difficult to see anything. Walking around the perimeter of his cottage afforded no signs of life—not even a trail of seeds or nuts.

I was worried because I was certain that something terrible had happened to Harold. For all I knew, he could be dead. I shuddered at the thought. Who could I possibly check in with to find out about him? I supposed that I could start knocking on doors along Lake Road, but the area was already looking vacated for the winter, and besides, did I really want to do that in this cold weather?

And then, quite miraculously, I thought of Violet. Surely, of all people, Violet would know something and I drove quickly through the barren, snowy landscape to Kincardine. It was nearing late afternoon. The green vines on Violet's window had faded since I'd been there last, but the familiar jingle rang out as I opened the door. Interestingly, the water fountains were silent and I could not smell any incense. *Maybe those are touches she only keeps up in the summer*, I decided. The store was reassuringly warm, though, and I treasured the heat while unwrapping my scarf from my neck.

A very slender girl was at the cash. "Hello. May I help you with anything?" She was incredibly soft spoken and kept her delicate hands clasped in front of her.

"I'm actually here because I was hoping to speak to Violet. Is she in?"

"No, sorry, not today. Is there anything I can help you with?"

The concept of privacy entered my mind and I wasn't sure what to say. Maybe this was none of my business. The girl was watching me with concerned eyes, so I finally relented. "Well, I wanted to ask about a resident on Lake Road. I used to have a cottage up here and I met this nice gentleman and I think he may have become sick. He doesn't appear to be at his house anymore, and I'm just… uh… sort of worried about him."

The girl adjusted some pens that were sitting beside the cash register. "Do you know his name? Perhaps I can help you."

What the heck, I decided. *I've come all this way.* "It's… um… Harold McKay."

As soon as I said his name she smiled, which was reassuring. "Oh, yes. He's a very nice man from what I hear. He's been in the hospital, though. I think he had a stroke."

I wasn't entirely surprised to hear this. I also wasn't surprised that she knew about Harold's health situation, given that in small towns like this one, people generally knew when something happened to someone. As it turned out, this girl's mother used to clean Harold's house. Despite my initial relief at having some answers, I was extremely sad to hear how quickly Harold had declined since our carefree summer day at the beach. I thanked the shop girl and went out in search of more information. I eventually struck it lucky at Finchers, the local book store, where the clerk told me that Harold had been transferred from the hospital to the Sunset Nursing Home a few blocks away.

It was beginning to get dark out when I drove up to Sunset a few minutes later. I was struck by the perfectly manicured shrubs and the beautiful arrangement of white Christmas lights that adorned each and every one of them. There was a large glass-encased lobby, and inside, several gray-haired individuals sat in wheelchairs or on benches. Their eyes were distant and empty. Occasionally the personal support worker who sat beside them would mumble something and point—perhaps to the lights or a squirrel—but the resident only continued to stare. There was an unnerving stillness to the place.

I walked up to the main entrance and felt the sadness of the residence penetrate me. The few residents that I passed didn't even bother to look up; it was as if they had already given up and surrendered to some invisible adversary. I wondered what kind of images passed through their minds. Were they constantly reminiscing about their first jobs at Birch Tree Resort and wiggling their toes in the sand? And yet, for others, perhaps there were no good memories.

The receptionist was chatty, and told me that my timing wasn't perfect. "Mr. McKay is only up for visitors for a short period in the late afternoon, and after that he becomes intolerable and is put to bed right after dinner. Even so, I don't think you'll be having any meaningful conversations with the man, if you know what I mean." She then proceeded to rant about how all the residents were extremely fatigued by dinnertime, and how it was a 'damn shit pain' to get enough nurses and support workers on staff to manage the evening shift.

"We've gone through two managers in six months, and the union reps will be down our backs in no time." She managed to sputter all of this while simultaneously sorting files, stapling papers, and paper clipping, her enormous hoop earrings moving in unison the whole time. I had to admit, she looked rather efficient.

Finally she pointed me in the direction of Harold's room. "And don't forget to use the hand sanitizer, okay?" She was chewing gum with her mouth open as she pointed to a small bottle on the corner of the counter. "The last thing we need in this place is another outbreak of Norwalk." I reached out to clean my hands when she suddenly yelled across the room, which made me jump out of my skin. "Mr. Batten! How many times have I told you to stay away from that fish tank? Did you hear me?"

Mr. Batten?

My eyes widened in surprise as she swivelled her chair one hundred and eighty degrees, stood up, and began stomping her way across the lobby. She was wearing a pair of tall black boots, and they squeaked as she pounced on the floor towards him. It all happened within a matter of seconds. She was as quick as lightning, and before I could blink, her hands made contact with the handles of the elderly gentleman's wheelchair and she yanked the occupant backwards. "Don't you remember what happened last time? Next time you get close to it, I'll have you back in your room. Got that, Mr. Batten?"

I was mortified. I wasn't sure if it was the name she'd just called him or the actual scene I'd witnessed.

"God damn these old people," she muttered as she sat back on her chair so hard that the air seeped out like a whistle in the wind.

I could think of nothing to say as I turned and started down the hallway. My hands had started to shake. As I made my way towards room three sixty-two, I felt queasy. I'd come here to see Harold, and yet the name Batten had just unleashed a wave of curiosity. There was a part of me that desperately wanted to meet my Jaime's loving grandfather, and yet he didn't know me. For all I knew, he could have dementia and any surprise visit would be a complete waste of time. He was, after all, in his eighties or nineties. And then there seemed to be that problem with the fish tank. Maybe he didn't have all of his marbles anymore.

And yet, after a brief connection with Harold, who snored his way through nearly my entire visit, I found myself creeping towards Mr. Batten's room. I stood in his open doorway and found him sitting in his wheelchair, facing the window with his back towards me. There was a little grey squirrel on his window sill, and someone had placed a wreath on the window that blinked every thirty seconds or so.

He appeared to be a tall man, and his posture and skeletal system hadn't betrayed him in his later years. There was still an abundance of gray hair on his head, and strong, bony hands grasped the edges of his arm rests.

After a brief hesitation, I knocked. There was no response, so I knocked again, louder this time. Without looking from the window, he raised his hand and made a movement that I could only interpret as meaning for me to enter. I entered the room and sat down on a chair that was facing him. He looked at me briefly before turning away again. I thought I saw him flinch, but I couldn't be entirely sure. His face had a vacancy similar to the folks I'd seen when I'd first entered the building.

I searched for any signs of Jaime in his face. *He is definitely old.* Skin sagged from the corners of his eyes and under his chin. He had a slight olive tint to his skin, and his eyes were a beautiful shade of hazel. He also had an edge to his features that made him still attractive in his later years. He wasn't too thin, or too heavy, and his broad shoulders held an aura of authority similar to those of a soldier.

Just as I opened my mouth to greet him and introduce myself, a nurse entered his room. "How nice, Mr. Batten. I see you have a visitor." She placed some supplies on his bedside table before tapping him on the shoulder. "You be nice now, you hear me? Or this pretty little lady won't come back." She laughed as she proceeded to exit his room, and I immediately felt uncomfortable.

"Hello, Mr. Batten. I hope I'm not bothering you. My name is Ann."

There was no response. Although he had flinched earlier, his eyes didn't even seem to register my presence now; they continued staring out the window.

I tried speaking louder. "Mr. Batten? It's nice to meet you! My name is Ann!"

Still, there was nothing. I could only surmise that dementia had hit him hard. Either that, or he simply had no interest in speaking to a stranger. I probably should have asked about his history at the front desk or, at the very least, tried to engage in conversation with the nurse.

We sat in silence for a few more minutes. I could tell that this visit was going nowhere, and I immediately felt foolish for having come to his room in the first place. I got up and scanned the room for a place to clean my hands. I washed them quickly, and as I wiped them dry, the old man's deep voice interrupted the crushing silence.

"Ann? Ann Ralston?"

I froze. How did he know my last name?

CHAPTER 40

Mr. Batten's voice paralyzed me. My crunched-up paper towel remained in my grasp, and I was frozen solid in my tracks.

"Are you Ann Ralston? I was hoping to meet you."

I swallowed hard, turned, and walked back to the chair I'd just vacated. As I slowly sat down, he turned and looked at me.   "Did Violet send you?" There was an edge to his voice now, and his apparent intrigue vanished.

"No," I said. The paper towel was still in my hands. *Violet?* How did he know Violet? And were we talking about the same Violet?

He turned his eyes back to the window, and my eyes followed his. The squirrel finally jumped from the ledge.

I felt I had to explain my presence, but I didn't know where on earth to start. "Nobody sent me. I came to see you because I… well, I used to own a cottage on Lake Road, next to this fellow named Jaime…Jaime Batten, and I… uh… I met this man named Harold McKay, and he told me all about Birch Tree Resort… and, well, I was here visiting him, and…"

His hand went up in the air, effectively stopping my words mid-stream. It was so archaic, this gesture from the past, and yet I obeyed. Another silence continued for what seemed like an eternity. By this point, I was becoming clammy. *How does he know who I am?* I began planning my exit again, but he must have sensed it because within seconds he was engaging me again.

"Jaime Batten is my grandson." He turned to look at me. His eyes were suddenly strong and sharp, and I felt like a knife had just pierced me. I shifted my weight in the chair, but managed to maintain eye contact. "Yes, he's my grandson as far as anyone is concerned. But he is not my blood, Ann."

My heart skipped a beat. I was surprised to hear this. When Harold had told me about Jaime Senior's trip to Detroit to adopt Robert, I just figured that he had to be the biological father—especially after reading the obituary. More importantly, why was he telling me this? I began to feel more and more frightened in this man's presence.

"I don't understand." It came out like a whisper.

I had to break his gaze and my eyes fell to his hands. I watched how his hands became tense and tightly gripped the hand rests of his wheelchair. He finally looked away towards the window, which afforded some relief on my end. The wreath blinked over and over again and it seemed like an eternity before he finally spoke again. When he did, his words were like fire spewing from his lips. "Mia Stohm was the biological mother of my adopted son Robert." He paused and cleared his throat again. "Mia was raped, Ann. She was brutally raped at the Birch Tree Resort on the very first night of their family vacation. The rumour about me fathering her child was one of many."

His statement took me by complete and utter surprise. Why was he sharing this with me? How could he possibly know that I knew about Mia and the baby? Had he and Harold been talking during their days together at the nursing home? No, I couldn't believe that, given the mental state that Harold was in. Besides, it seemed like something much more cosmic was happening here. It's like we had begun this conversation years ago—eons ago, another lifetime ago—and we were picking it right back up again, without missing a beat.

"It happened behind the old well," he continued bitterly. "What a travesty. She was such a beautiful, sweet girl."

The ancient well came to mind. I'd seen it during my first visit to Birch Tree, and I easily recalled its beauty. How ironic that they had preserved the antiquity and charm of that structure, though it was home to a secret brutality as far as old man Batten was concerned.

My eyes were wide and riveted on this old man. There was more to this story than I ever could have guessed, and he was still not finished. Suddenly the whirring of the radiator at the far corner of the window sounded like a jet engine.

"You cannot be with young Jaime, Ann. Do you understand that?"

I felt the blood begin to drain from my face and extremities. *How the hell did the conversation jump to this topic? And how much does this man know about Jaime and me?*

The steely eyes turned on me again. "Do you know who raped Mia, Ann?"

I stared blankly at him. I couldn't feel my pulse. Something was terribly wrong, and even though the words had not yet been spoken, I could already taste their malevolence. I somehow managed to shake my head no.

"Do you remember your Great Uncle Stephen, Ann?"

I began to feel nauseous. The walls of the room were closing in on me. I looked up, dizzy. The open door to the hallway was only a few feet away and I thought about running. The whirring noise of the radiator stopped abruptly, and there was complete silence.

"He was twenty-one years old, Ann, and Mia was just a girl—she was just sixteen years old, and built like a bird. It was her very first night at the resort. It was after the bed call, and Mia had snuck outside for a cigarette. She never could have imagined…" He shook his head, as if trying to shake something loose inside.

"He tied her arms to the well ropes, and cranked them so hard he almost dislocated her shoulders. He tore off her pajamas and panties with his jack knife, then threw them down the well. He gagged her and told her that if she made any noise, he would cut her between her legs." There was another long pause, followed by a deep breath. His face suddenly became contorted, and he looked to be in some sort of physical pain. "He'd already violated her several times when I found her tied to that well three hours later. She was bleeding profusely. It was a miracle she didn't die."

He said no more, and there was nothing I could say. *My great uncle is Jaime's biological grandfather. My own flesh and blood caused this horror...* The facts were seeping in slowly, like a leak in an old tin boat. But my mind refused to register them. We sat in silence for what seemed like an eternity.

Then I stood up and walked out of the room. I knew then that I would never see Mr. Jaime Batten Senior again.

CHAPTER 41

There was a knowing. In fact, it had always been there, but I had somehow missed it. The water… the drive across the landscape… the eerie familiarity. It was all coming together now.

I was back in the city later that night. After a long drive with nothing to do except remember, it was all coming into focus. I was sitting at my kitchen table, old family photographs spread around me and my head in my hands. A mug of tea had already gone stone cold at my elbow without me having taken even a sip. I closed my eyes and the memories washed over me.

October had been uncharacteristically chilly that year, and there was a light, early snowfall dusting the landscapes. Alistair, my wonderful and loving grandfather, was sitting at the old kitchen table rolling tobacco in little white papers. I was four years old and methodically pulling each paper out of the little green Export package, one by one, and handing them to him. I remember telling him how I liked the little lady's beret on the canister, and he smiled. I watched how he carefully scooped out a teaspoon of brown bits from the tin, placed them in a small even pile on each paper, and tightly rolled a perfect cigarette. I was amazed at how precisely he worked, the small movements of his fingers working in complete harmony. On occasion, he would hand one over, and I felt privileged to lick the glue—a clean line across, the tingle on my tongue. There was an unmatched silence marred by the sound of the clock ticking loudly in the background. When I looked up at my grandfather Alistair, he smiled. It was a hearty, reassuring smile that always gave me a warm, spreading feeling in my stomach. He was reaching out to pat my head like he always did.

But his hand never reached me that day, because just then, a shotgun was fired, twice, the first shot shattering the kitchen window. The noise was deafening, and I felt some small stabs of pain as pieces of glass pierced my skin. My grandfather acted quickly, pushing me violently against the floor, yelling for me to get down and descending upon me like an enormous shield.

It wasn't until many years later, when I was much older and I could understand, that I learned Grandpa Al's brother, Stephen, had supposedly committed suicide in the back shed that day. Mother always said that if Uncle Stephen had known I was in the kitchen, he never would have shot near the house that day. They even wondered if he'd just run into trouble when trying to orient the gun into his mouth and the shot was misfired accidentally.

And yet, others in the family thought differently. They said that Grandpa was Uncle Stephen's target because he had been the source of

Stephen's angst for many years leading up to that day. They had argued that it wasn't a suicide. The rumours continued to be sketchy, but some argued that although Stephen appeared to be a relatively normal man to outsiders, he was deeply retarded in capacity. Terms like schizophrenia and manic-depressive were thrown around, and still others said that it was because he had been severely abused by a neighbour as a child.

I picked up a picture of Aunt Eleanor, my mother's sister, from the pile. She was wearing her turquoise cat-eye glasses with a yellow kerchief tied neatly around her neck. She was smoking a cigarette and held a package of Rothman's in her other hand. *Uncle Stephen is a psycho. You keep him away from the children, Elsa, or you'll be sorry.*

We had been at some lake. It was a rented cottage right on the water that our families had used for many years up until the time Uncle Stephen killed himself. The details were all coming back to me now. Aunt Eleanor had been speaking with my mother at the time, her hand waving and drawing smoke across the cottage kitchen as her cigarette dangled from her fingers. Although I had no idea what the word psycho meant, I immediately followed the cues of my mother, who quickly dismissed Eleanor with a roll of her eyes.

I stared down at the pictures and could vaguely recall now that mother had boasted of Grandpa Al and Uncle Stephen. They had secured jobs at a swanky resort near our rented cottage, but she'd never told me its name. Or had she? As I scanned the photos that lay before me and simultaneously searched my vault of memories, one image eventually emerged. I picked up a photo that had been folded down the middle, and one of its corners had been cut. I held it up to the light and stared at Grandpa Al standing proudly with his arm around Great Uncle Stephen. Was the fold a coincidence, or truly symbolic of separation? My eyes searched the photograph for clues. They were both so handsome, standing in front of a grand Lincoln with a young, pretty girl in the background. She had an eerie, frightened look in her eyes. I recalled asking my mother about the girl when I was much younger. *Oh, Ann, I don't know. Probably a daughter of someone. What does it matter?*

And yet it did matter, for on the back of the photo was written 1947—the same year that Mia won the beauty contest but had been raped. Now I could see how everything was starting to make sense. It was Birch Tree Resort, and it was the year that Mia had become pregnant.

As I stared at that photo of Mia in the Lincoln, I couldn't help but see the resemblance. She looked like Jaime.

CHAPTER 42

My research was thorough. There were multiple trips and reconnections, and my relatives were more than overjoyed to catch up. But it was the critical visit with my mother that changed everything. At first she didn't want to discuss anything, but with my dogged persistence, I was finally able to get her to speak.

She told me how, in 1947, Uncle Stephen had been hired by Birch Tree Resort as a janitor. There had been an initial reluctance to hire him because he came off as a somewhat unlikeable character, but eventually a soft heart had emerged and the owners told him that if he did well over the summer, he could be promoted to the kitchen. Grandpa had been in charge of the grounds, and as I learned, it was he who had discovered Mia's panties and pyjamas in the well and buried them in the garden. Whatever may have gone through his mind during that horrible summer will never be known, but he certainly made decisions that would stay with him forever—and that set a course of events that would eventually lead to Stephen reaching for a rifle many years later. It was difficult to comprehend how Grandpa had held onto those dark secrets, and still managed to be so jovial—or, at least, *seem* to be jovial to those around him.

My mother went on to tell me stories her own mother had shared with her. Stephen had been known to move about the resort at a snail's pace—just the opposite of my grandfather, who had been promoted for his quick and effective work. Wearing dark gray overalls even in the thick heat, Stephen would pick up and examine bits of garbage from the grounds before finally making some decision to part with it and throw it in the trash cans. While the young women frolicked or played croquet, he would stare at them, his body quivering, from behind the trash bins. I could imagine that those girls would have stirred Stephen to no end, and I could almost picture his foul mouth salivating at the perky breasts that peeked out of their polka-dotted halter tops.

Stephen was a loner, and he had no friends except for Grandpa Al. According to my mother, Grandpa had apparently played a huge role in blaming Mia's pregnancy on the half-Huron boy, Jaime Batten. He would have done this out of loyalty, of course, and to protect the family name and his only brother.

Why had she never told me about this rape in our family? As I sat at home on a cold, gray night and thought about all of this, I reached up to touch my face and realized that I had no tears left. *There are some secrets that are never shared, she told me.* Her words were curt and I felt betrayed. My mind went to Jaime's grandfather—the man who'd stoically taken the blame for it all, and then done what no one else had been prepared to do and raised Mia's child as his own, amid the ghosts of Huron shores.

Huron ghosts… and Huron shame. My *family's* shame.

***

Weeks passed by, and when Christmas Eve arrived, I drove out of the city in search of the church that I had passed countless times during my many trips to Heart House. Inglewood Church stood on the side of the highway. Its Gothic-style windows were set within a framework of polychromatic stonework, and the enormous copper steeple captured the attention of every passerby. This was the first time I mounted the steps of this beautiful building, and I wondered what had taken me so long.

An original cast iron coal lamp hung solemnly in the front entrance. It was almost midnight, and I knew no one at the service. The back pew was vacant, and as I sat down in the dark shadows, I held a small cross and asked for absolution. I wasn't sure what was worse—the ties of consanguinity between Jaime and I, or the filth of my ancestral past.

When my cell phone rang over and over on Christmas morning, I watched it vibrate across my kitchen table but didn't answer the calls. I only stared out the window at the falling snow and the gray sky. I placed my hand on the cold window pane and watched how my fingers slowly formed an impression on the glass. Jaime and I had discovered a beautiful yet chaotic love dance, but we were tainted by the past. It simply could never be.

My hand dropped slowly from the window. I could only hope that the cycle of separation and connection would find us once again in another lifetime.

CHAPTER 43

No one expected the record snowfalls that winter, and despite the harshness of the hinterland, the sun occasionally managed to peek through and make the snow sparkle like diamonds. A brisk wind was constantly skirting through Grey Bruce Township, and the wind turbines responded in unison. Snowflakes danced amongst the wooden cottage porches, only to nestle among the ancient cobwebs once the wind had subsided.

No one would have expected to see young Jaime Batten sitting by the water's edge in a state of calm bliss on Christmas morning. He had returned home in high spirits, for he had just made a very difficult decision. Although it had taken several years for him to come to terms with it, he was willing to take a chance and grow with the precious gift that had been given to him. It was a grave decision that he knew his grandfather would never approve of, but Jaime chose to defy ethics and play out a terrible sin with someone he loved. There would be no more lies or hiding. And, most importantly, he wouldn't have to hold back any longer; he didn't think he'd be able to, even if he tried.

Four years earlier, he had used his police connections to conduct a thorough investigation of Ann

Ralston, his new potential neighbour, and had been shocked to discover the ancestral link. He had consulted with his grandfather, who told him what he knew about Stephen Ralston's violent connection to the Stohm and Batten families. Consequently, Jaime had done his best to forestall Ann's purchase of the property. But he had lost.

He had been extremely guarded on the day that she'd arrived. He'd glanced momentarily towards Heart House while he had worked on his catamaran, and he couldn't help but wonder if his hesitance was unjustified and presumptuous. After all, two whole generations had passed since then.

It wasn't until he walked down to the beach on that beautiful sunny day and met her that he knew his reservations had been unjustified. He was struck the minute he saw her; as he later told his friend Siobhan, Ann jarred his senses in a way that scared him. He had felt an immediate connection to her, and it frightened him.

From that day on, in accordance with Siobhan's advice and his grandfather's warnings, he had done everything in his power to ignore her—and yet he'd wanted to be near her so badly. To talk with her. To laugh with her. To enjoy life with her. He had lain awake many a night in fits of despair, constantly alternating between his moral obligations and his own deep yearnings.

Although he'd felt drawn to her, his frequent visits to the nursing home to see his grandfather fuelled the notion that Ann and he could never be. Jaime had agonized over his feelings, and at one point had even considered the option of holding out until his grandfather died, but on further reflection, he realized that he couldn't do it. He couldn't disobey his grandfather in that way—a man who had been so utterly betrayed by the Ralston brothers, though he had borne it in silence.

He'd had no choice but to concoct the ridiculous story about his sexuality. He'd instantly regretted it the moment the words had been out of his mouth. It was a cover story he'd grown so comfortable with over the past months that it had seemed only natural to hide within it once again. Remembering back to the night of their first kiss pained him beyond description. He'd put his fist through an upstairs window and cursed at the moon. But that was all he had been able to do. And so he'd left.

His work had kept him busy, and the odd moments of gunfire had relieved him of his grief. On other nights, he surrendered to black dreams and clawed at his bed sheets. But it was the fateful trip to Grand Cayman that changed everything. It was there, hundreds of miles away from Lake Huron, where he ultimately decided that Ann and he were meant to be together. How else could he explain the heavens and stars working so valiantly to create a chance meeting like that?

Despite the fact that Ann's great uncle was also his grandfather, Jaime made the most important decision of his life: to forgo the consanguinity connection. Marrying a first cousin was quite acceptable in other parts of the world, and had been the norm right up until the 1900s even in Canada. So why should he let the fact that he and Ann were distant cousins stand in the way of their happiness? Enough social conventions had stood in the way of his family's happiness—his grandfather had been chastised and vilified for being half Huron, and the break-up of his biological mother and his father had been the talk of the town. And yet, he somehow knew that it was the *brutality* of the conception, and not the consanguinity, that would be the real issue for Ann. At least, it had been so for his grandfather.

So as he waited for Ann on Christmas morning, sitting by the shore and thinking about their future together, he became more and more convinced that the wrongdoings of their ancestors could be rectified. Once again, life had come full circle to make the necessary amendments.

Jaime waited all day for Ann, and he called her repeatedly. The air was cool, and as he stared out to the horizon, he thought he knew what was coming. From time to time his eyes would check his watch, however, as time wore on, his smile would slowly fade even further from his face. Eventually, his hope left him, just like the sun left Lake Huron at the end of the day.

He picked himself up and left the shore, his hands thrust deep into his pockets, walking slowly towards his house in the dark. A burst of wind picked up just as he passed by Heart House. That little cottage, once so full of promise, was now dark and empty except for the memories. A small pile of wood and garbage lay near the edge of the driveway, lit by an outside light. As Jaime peered closely, the wooden heart that used to hang on the door came into view. It was covered with a combination of garbage, black ash, and pine needles. The new owners must have thrown it out.

Jaime stood on Lake Road, unmoving. After a moment, however, he kneeled down and picked up the worn, weather-beaten heart. He carefully tucked it in his jacket pocket, promising himself that he'd return the following spring to nail it back on the door, where it was meant to be.

EPILOGUE

The bells chimed as the last customer left the store. Her aged hands carefully pulled down a shutter and turned over a placard in the window to display the closed sign. She blew out the candles and incense and walked over to a small display by the window that showcased an array of carved animals. She picked up a bear and examined the intricate carving, tracing her fingers along the edges that framed its face. She placed it next to her heart and remembered watching how his hands had worked with precision and ease.

She recalled her conversation with Robert, the only man she had loved. "Can you do that, too?"

He had smiled while delicately tucking a piece of her hair behind her ear. "Not as good as my father can." Tears formed at the corner of her eyes. She recalled how Robert's emotions were always scarred by an absent mother. It had played out over and over again in the early part of their relationship ultimately leading to their separation.

She carefully placed the bear back on the shelf and closed her eyes. She thought of Jaime. Little Jaime.

Her beautiful son.

She knew he had left Kincardine, and that nobody had seen him for a long, long time. The locals said his free spirit was no more.

But Violet knew different. The veil of darkness had finally been lifted. If his spirit had departed, she knew it would return some day. It always did.

She blew out the last candle and smiled.

ACKNOWLEDGEMENTS

What a journey this book has taken since 2009! Working full time, running a small business on the side, and keeping up with the demands of a family meant this book took last place on my list of priorities. And yet it gave me immense pleasure when I was immersed in the writing. The plot and characters unfolded in a miraculous way; I was captivated by the plot, and in the end, I was very happy with the final result.

Had it not been for the subtle encouragement of a few individuals (who eagerly wanted to read the story), it would never have been shared and ultimately printed. It was my own personal treasure and I had no intention of this story going anywhere beyond the hard drive of my laptop!

Thus, I am incredibly grateful to the following individuals that pushed me to the next level: Barbara Cawley, Alla Gower, Nadine Lucki, Jane Pitchford Bartsch, Helen Wright Francia, and Betty Yu. All of these women took time out of their extremely busy schedules to read this story, give me honest feedback and most importantly, encouraged me to go to print. Because of them, I persevered on a journey that I never imagined would come true. Thank you to all of you from the bottom of my heart.

An enormous thank you also goes out to my editor, Elizabeth Bond. I thank my lucky stars for finding her as she did an incredible job of finding flaws that I was blind to.

Last but not least, I wish to thank my family for enduring all those long (dazed) hours I spent on the computer. You are the three most important people in my life, and I bless and thank the heavens every day that I have you.

REFERENCES

www.philosophicalsociety.com &
www.parkridgecentre.org
An Existential View on Loneliness by Michele A. Carter
Canadian House & Home (for having the perfect
cottage picture/description that became the interior
setting of Heart House)
www.claudechurch.com
Inglewood church is fictitious but based on Claude
Presbyterian Church that resides in Caledon, Ontario.
www.caymanislands.ky
www.sunsets.com
www.thebrucepeninsula.com
A Lover's Fool by Derell Bosworth
www.limekilncottages.com
Birch Tree Resort is fictitious and loosely based on the
'Lime Kiln Resort' which resides on the shores of Lake
Huron at Inverhuron Beach. Some of the original
newsletters from the 1950s can be viewed on their
website.
www.wikipedia.com
www.inspirationpeak.com